U0081570

陳秀珍 著
Poems by Chen Hsiu-chen

李魁賢 譯
Translated by Lee Kuei-shien

親愛的
聶魯達

My Beloved
Neruda

陳秀珍漢英雙語詩集
Mandarin-English

台灣詩叢 • Taiwan Poetry Series 13

【總序】詩推台灣意象

叢書策劃／李魁賢

　　進入21世紀，台灣詩人更積極走向國際，個人竭盡所能，在詩人朋友熱烈參與支持下，策劃出席過印度、蒙古、古巴、智利、緬甸、孟加拉、馬其頓等國舉辦的國際詩歌節，並編輯《台灣心聲》等多種詩選在各國發行，使台灣詩人心聲透過作品傳佈國際間。接續而來的國際詩歌節邀請愈來愈多，已經有應接不暇的趨向。

　　多年來進行國際詩交流活動最困擾的問題，莫如臨時編輯帶往國外交流的選集，大都應急處理，不但時間緊迫，且選用作品難免會有不週。因此，興起策劃【台灣詩叢】雙語詩系的念頭。若台灣詩人平常就有雙語詩集出版，隨時可以應用，詩作交流與詩人交誼雙管齊下，更具實際成效，對台灣詩的國際交流活動，當更加順利。

　　以【台灣】為名，著眼點當然有鑑於台灣文學在國際間名目不彰，台灣詩人能夠有機會在國際努力開拓空間，非為個人建立知名度，而是為推展台灣意象的整體事功，期待開創台灣文學的長久景象，才能奠定寶貴的歷史意義，台灣文學終必在世界文壇上佔有地位。

　　實際經驗也明顯印證，台灣詩人參與國際詩交流活動，很受重視，帶出去的詩選集也深受歡迎，從近年外國詩人和出版社與本人合作編譯台灣詩選，甚至主動翻譯本人詩集在各國文學雜誌或詩刊發表，進而出版外譯詩集的情況，大為增多，即可充分證明。

　　承蒙秀威資訊科技公司一本支援詩集出版初衷，慨然接受【台灣詩叢】列入編輯計畫，對台灣詩的國際交流，提供推進力量，希望能有更多各種不同外語的雙語詩集出版，形成進軍國際的集結基地。

2017.02.15誌

目次

朝聖愛情

——序陳秀珍《親愛的聶魯達》

林鷺

　　愛情自古至今是一個既陳舊又新鮮的話題。愛情的陳義有時高貴有時卑微；愛情的試煉有時偉大，有時殘酷。愛情多麼讓人仰望，卻也常常讓人在卻步中嘆息。有人好奇愛情的詩篇一旦產量過多，詩是否容易像失色的玫瑰花，既無色澤也無芳香。這個疑問從詩人陳秀珍以愛情為標誌，持續不斷的創作中，得到讓人吃驚的答案。且說，世人總愛稱頌諾貝爾文學獎得主，智利詩人聶魯達的愛情詩，數不清的詩人前仆後繼，努力嘗試也來攀登聶魯達出自天性建構的情詩高峰。當一位崇尚愛情的女詩人，終於在2018年親自踏上聶魯達出生成長的國土，拜訪聶魯達曾經住過的三個居所，誰不好奇她總計66首的《親愛的聶魯達》詩集，寫下的會是什麼樣的情詩？

　　莎士比亞曾經在《仲夏夜之夢》裡，說過：「瘋子、情人、詩人都是想像的產兒。」的確，愛情的詩句總是在想像中產生。詩人情意深刻淋漓的傳達，萃取了詩豐富的想像力，我以此看待陳秀珍的智利之行，毋寧是一場屬於她的愛情朝聖。旅程從「聶魯達／我懼怕／像海浪愛海岸岩礁／那般愛你／擊碎自己」的忐忑呢喃中，飛抵詩人們所嚮往的〈聶魯達的天空〉。

　　詩人攜帶她心中的愛情從天空著陸，如願溫柔在「夕陽仿冒

紅燈」的時光裡，也從「聶魯達啊／在智利奇妙時空／你用你的
母語／我用我的母語／雙重朗讀一首情詩」的〈雙重唱〉掀起序
幕，讓愛在「夜／讓身體勃發嫩芽」的激情中，委身聶魯達黑島
故居面海〈海風冷冷〉的衝突裡，成為呼喊：「聶魯達啊／我向
你呼求必需的養分／芽要獻祭自己／變成一朵馥郁玫瑰／紅給黑
島／香給春天」的謙卑情人。

　　愛情的獻祭總是從情愛的擁抱中開始，以下這首：

〈在你的擁抱中〉

　　在你的擁抱中
　　我成為一隻小船
　　放棄風與帆
　　偎依你溫柔的港灣

　　在你的擁抱中
　　我成為一隻溫馴白鴿
　　放棄整片天空
　　你就是我的翅膀

　　在你的擁抱中
　　我迷失方向
　　我用你兩把眼睛的火炬

在無盡長夜為我導航

在你的擁抱中
我全身化為一隻耳朵
我聽不見萬獸朝我嘶吼
專聽你對我竊竊耳語

在你的擁抱中
我自動繳出槍與彈
你有最厲害的武器
我情願為你負傷累累

聶魯達啊
我用僅有的生命
交換你
一個情意無限的擁抱

詩人滿懷濃烈的情意，甚且願意以「我的夢境無須繁瑣簽證／只須自由心證／我許你自由入境／百次／千回」──〈薄暮〉的詩句，來應許她給予愛情的無限寬容。

陳秀珍詩的意象向來繁複多變，詩的情感意深情濃，語言且不流於艱澀。基本上，我認為閱讀她的詩，很容易就被她滿溢的詩情所吸引。姑且讓我略舉以下幾例做為明證：

「醉了／木頭人的我／想要變成豐滿葡萄／被醞釀／變成一瓶／高酒精含量紅酒」──〈葡萄紅酒〉

「耳環遺落／還給耳垂自由／為什麼耳朵還不時聽見／叮叮噹噹／耳環迴響」──〈耳環〉

「想像繁星／是你微笑的眼睛／一眨眼飛濺出來的水晶碎片／黏貼在黑緞天幕／從此／我愛黑夜勝過白天」──〈繁星〉

「初春深宵／套上層層冬衣／像一顆洋蔥／埋進黑壤的厚被／等待旭日／讓我發芽」──〈寒〉

「曖昧的愛／是幸福的／請勿用你耳語／你的咒語／接生我的愛」──〈愛〉

愛情如果只帶來簡單的幸福，想必情感未必深刻，更或許不可能有值得歌頌的情詩產生。陳秀珍著墨的愛情詩，具備愛情應有的所有元素。例如〈夢〉裡的「聶魯達啊／夢的獠牙嚼完整夜星空／轉頭嚼食／亞當捨給我的肋骨／使我有說不出的／痛」；〈前進駱馬城〉的「聶魯達啊／我不成為流不到海的那湖／不成為只會發呆的樹／越過多少寂寞落日／總算來到詩人之國／若你是岩山／我就化成種籽／種進你身體／成為你的骨」，以及〈薄紫〉的「午夜／我被風吹進你的夢歷險／明明你掛起弓與箭／我卻遍體鱗傷」「聶魯達啊／不勞而獲的獵人／我須在你靈魂深處／療傷」等，都把愛情刻骨銘心的焦慮、痛苦與哀傷，以詩美麗的意象送達讀者的肺腑。

　　然而，我要提醒的是，讀者看待陳秀珍的情詩，不能只設限在男女情愛的想像，因為她情詩伸展的觸角具有特殊的廣度。她有能力把吸收來的各種情境，以不同型式的語言轉化成情感豐富的詩情。我從這本詩集也讀到她以愛情伸展的腳步。例如：詩人參觀智利第一位諾貝爾獎得主米斯特拉爾的故居，就寫下：「愛情／比諾貝爾文學獎更難獲得／妳在死亡的十四行／淌下熱淚多少行／我偷偷為妳拭去憂傷／妳的淚濕了／我的心」──〈米斯特拉爾故居〉；參訪智利創造主義倡議者詩人文森・維多夫羅的墓園後，也以這位詩人生前〈詩藝〉一詩的結句──「詩人是一位小小上帝」轉折成「詩人／你是一位小小上帝／我願／活在你的創世紀」的〈夢境〉；或是寫給智利詩人奧斯卡・卡斯特羅的「在月下在百合花香中／你的孤獨／確確實實親吻了／我的孤獨／我將玫瑰獻上／陪伴你／深深的睡眠」──〈我將玫瑰獻上〉等，都是她以愛情為基調的詩人之愛的愛情詩。

　　我也注意到陳秀珍從國家之愛出發的愛情詩寫得並不少，屢次以詩出訪交流的她，並沒有忘記自己的國家。〈慕光2〉就出現以下這樣的一段詩句：

　　聶魯達啊
　　你在安穩的生活中
　　西班牙在你心中
　　你是一點螢光
　　對抗巨大黑暗

> 在你螢光中
> 我思考
> 如何成為一隻螢火蟲
> 台灣在我心中

　　陳秀珍猶如一座裝滿能量，持續噴發的愛情活火山，她不僅寫下不少值得戀愛中，或已經遺忘愛情的人，所閱讀的情詩；對於那位被愛情之國所朝聖的情詩之王聶魯達，一旦發現遙遠的東方，居然有位才情橫溢的女詩人，以同樣震顫心弦的詩句，唱和他所歌頌的愛情，眼睛想必會噙著感動的淚水。我不知道哪位詩人曾經說過：「人生是一幅風景，愛情是一束鮮花。沒有鮮花，風景就不會絢麗，沒有愛情，人生就容易成為荒涼的土地。」我僅以詩人在這本詩集〈天涯之國〉詩中的一段詩句：

> 在人生中途
> 你用詩照亮我的地圖
> 如果不是遇見你
> 此刻我會在哪裡
> 如果不是遇見你
> 我會朝聖哪一顆星

　　來祝福這世界上的所有人，都能在生命的旅程，順利找到屬於自己所朝聖的那一顆愛情星！

聶魯達的天空

風
撕掉一葉葉
紅楓張貼的秋天告示
我心在絕望中
傾聽你情詩百首

春天在遠方
我恍惚聽見
誰在聲聲呼喚

心中密藏一座海洋
從島嶼台灣
飛向聶魯達的天空
高調頌讚
情詩十四行

聶魯達
我愛你
像勿忘我愛戀五月

聶魯達
我懼怕
像海浪愛海岸岩礁
那般愛你
擊碎自己

2018.10

十月在智利

十月
迎向意外恩典
秋風中我滿手落葉
閉目遙想太平洋另一岸
春光浪漫

你濤聲激昂的黑島*1
你留下許多秋波的聖地亞哥*2
你遺世的瓦爾帕來索*3
會是我暫時的避難所？

聶魯達啊
我的腳步聲將成為
你居所短暫的收藏

甦醒千樹萬草
智利之春

將初版何種花色情書
擱淺我
撩亂的眼神
悸動的心

*¹黑島有聶魯達故居。
*²聖地亞哥有聶魯達故居。
*³瓦爾帕來索有聶魯達故居。

2018.10

雙重唱

夕陽仿冒紅燈
掛在天空
夜間
海面像凝固的天色
天空影印白色海潮

聶魯達啊
在智利奇妙時空
你用你的母語
我用我的母語
雙重朗讀一首情詩

像此刻
海面與天空互譯
海潮音共鳴
兩心深谷

2018.10

白鹿

三年前
日月潭畔
我用盛開的耳朵閱讀
異國詩人朗詩
花香瀰漫中
我微顫的手捕獲一隻
藏身萬葉間
詩意的白鹿

此刻
我輕聲朗讀自己的詩
驚詫中
我捕獲
一度遺失的那白鹿

聶魯達啊
我害怕

我失而復得的白鹿
再度埋入雲霧重重歧途
我害怕
我的白鹿眷戀雲霧

我雙目
升起兩潭雲霧
白鹿白鹿
莫再棄我
於不顧

2018.10

在你的擁抱中

在你的擁抱中
我成為一隻小船
放棄風與帆
偎依你溫柔的港灣

在你的擁抱中
我成為一隻溫馴白鴿
放棄整片天空
你就是我的翅膀

在你的擁抱中
我迷失方向
我用你兩把眼睛的火炬
在無盡長夜為我導航

在你的擁抱中
我全身化為一隻耳朵

我聽不見萬獸朝我嘶吼
專聽你對我竊竊耳語

在你的擁抱中
我自動繳出槍與彈
你有最厲害的武器
我情願為你負傷累累

聶魯達啊
我用僅有的生命
交換你
一個情意無限的擁抱

2018.11
《笠》329期，2019年2月

海風冷冷

海風冷冷
灌進毛孔
灌進呼吸道
把我凍結成
一棵徹頭徹尾清醒的樹

夜
身體勃發嫩芽

聶魯達啊
我向你呼求必需的養分
芽要獻祭自己
變成一朵馥郁玫瑰
紅給黑島
香給春天

耳語

白花
飄飛似雪
高跟鞋咄咄
踩過一排花樹下
沾取奢華花香味

如幻聽
似咒語
勿忘我！勿忘我！勿忘我！
是花瓣在耳語
還是壓抑在我心底的聲音？

聶魯達啊
在聖地亞哥星光下
我心花開似雪
花瓣要飄降你心底

2018.10

忘我

不只白花
紅橙黃紫野花
也在春風鼓動中
爭相對我喃喃
喃喃
勿忘我！勿忘我！勿忘我！

不只浪花、海鳥
樹葉也在銀色月光下
向我低語
勿忘我！勿忘我！勿忘我！

不只山谷、丘陵
星、月、太陽
也向我不斷耳語
勿忘我！勿忘我！勿忘我！

聶魯達啊
全世界唯獨你
尚未忘我地向我表白
勿忘我呀
勿忘我

2018.10

聖地亞哥的眼睛

——在聶魯達故居

像佈下眼線
這裡那裡
眼睛無所不在

像嚴厲情人
獨裁的眼睛
在內室在花園
檢驗愛
堅不堅定

像被慾望綑綁
眼睛
尋尋覓覓
盲目愛情

聶魯達啊
那麼多隻不成雙的

眼睛眼睛眼睛

哪一隻是我

哪一隻是你

我們能組成一雙眼睛

凝望同一顆星嗎？

我想捕獲你

又怕

被你捕獲

*在聶魯達故居，室內外都有不少眼睛的圖騰。

2018.11

《笠》329期，2019年2月

耳環

耳環遺落
還給耳垂自由
為什麼耳朵還不時聽見
叮叮噹噹
耳環迴響

被耳洞拘留時
耳環見證
許許多多誓言
海枯石爛之前
耳環無智慧判斷
情人真心會不會枯爛

被思念
被呼喚
耳朵就會像急性發炎
那般發癢

耳環
習不習慣重獲自由
會不會朝夕思念
耳邊誓言

聶魯達啊
誓言是春風
耳環曾經等待
隨時被振動

2018.11
《笠》329期，2019年2月

薄暮

樹
高舉千手萬指
捕獲倦鳥

疏林
透出燈光的眼睛
偷窺
我們坐在車中數算
越來越多的眼睛
眼睛

如微小波浪的搖籃
輕輕搖晃的旅途
夜色成為有效護身符
我在尋求
頭顱倚靠的厚實肩膀
成為美夢溫床

聶魯達啊
我的夢境無須繁瑣簽證
只須自由心證
我許你自由入境
百次
千回

2018.11
《笠》329期，2019年2月。

塗鴉

在瓦爾帕萊索大斜坡
一條塗鴉街
塗滿花花綠綠
沒有憂鬱空隙
如拉美人
樂觀奔放心性

塗鴉
在一面一面牆壁
比賽訴說多彩的故事
即使老屋
也有青春面容
看不出老人斑

聶魯達啊
我車禍骨折
腿部留下一道暗紫傷疤

深深凹陷
像醜陋街巷
我該學習智利人
在傷疤上塗鴉
紅玫瑰花

2018.11

遮蔽

——黑島海鳥

在太平洋岸
我清楚聽見
一隻海鳥
清脆果決拍翅
宣告對天空火熱的愛

在黑島
她曾經捨棄整片天空
慌慌張張用雙翅遮蔽
害羞的臉
畏縮的腳

聶魯達啊
在你無際的藍空
你看不見
你可能也無法想像
她炫技的飛翔

2018.11

月出駱馬城

車子向海拔攀升
到達高山
比第一顆星早到

千萬顆星星都到齊
還等不到一輪滿月
有些星星沉睡了
有些星星感冒了
有些星星變成藍色

生起營火燒成太陽吧
用紅酒升高愛情熱度抵抗睡意吧
聶魯達啊
月亮拋棄整片天空了嗎？

我正要閉上眼目
放棄等待
等待被放棄的月亮

忽從遠山裂縫射出
純金光芒
啊
星星星星都哭了

滿月照亮
我童年被弦月割過的耳朵
月光逼出詩人原形
伸長脖子張開血盆大口
詩人發出狼嚎
震動駱馬山谷

未被狼群吞噬的金月
守護
駱馬城春夢

2018.11
《笠》329期，2019年2月

黑島

天空擁抱海洋
海洋親吻天堂

潮浪高亢激情的聲帶
無法掩蓋
你與愛人流動不已的腳步聲
掀開編織浪漫的白床單
枕頭留給潛入的朝陽
你連心跳都還清晰可聞

你怎能堅定信仰
隱藏在愛情裡的祕密
祕密是聖誕樹下
包裝在雲彩紙的神祕禮物
誘發每一隻手
偷窺的欲望

我闖進你原本私密的居所
聶魯達啊
告訴我
隱藏在愛情裡的祕密
我把耳朵打開
像天空那麼大

我聽見
滾滾海浪
不斷用裸體撞擊岩礁

2018.11
《笠》329期，2019年2月

紀念館

凝視
一張張被相機挽留的臉
相逢的臉
道別的臉

聽見
流連不已腳步聲
在黑島
野花占據春天的海角
在瓦爾帕萊索
彩屋拼圖的山坡
在聖地亞哥
裝飾許多眼睛的居所

魚
想拴住海浪腳步

海浪
卻不斷奔向無意的岸

聶魯達啊
我小小心房
變成一座龐雜紀念館
迷失的小鹿
莫再回頭
敲亂我心

2018.11

收藏

在滿室收藏中
你與愛人並肩坐在長桌邊
緊密相靠的椅子
分享溫熱咖啡
在甜蜜的晨光
在慵懶的黃昏
或許也分享些許憂傷
愛情總也塗染灰藍

在沒有你的居所
你曖昧的腳步聲
一步步向我逼近
為我導覽你蒐羅多年
摯愛收藏

我聽見愛情雙弦
共鳴如兩顆心悸動

我看見愛情在跳探戈
如玫瑰與自己的舞影

聶魯達啊
在你無盡的收藏
最教我忌妒
是你堅信的愛情
你的愛
不渝
在情詩字字句句裡
我想偷走
你一行愛情
讓我今天
融成金黃酒液

2018.11

葡萄紅酒

被時光醞釀的海洋
薄暮時
變成一潭色澤迷人的酒
醉了
我的眼

續杯紅酒
醉了
我的腸我的胃
我石質的心

醉了
木頭人的我
想要變成豐滿葡萄
被醞釀
變成一瓶
高酒精含量紅酒

聶魯達啊
將我飲下
讓我占有你
像一尾魚占有一座海洋

2018.11

笑

星星擠爆天空
海浪在海裡跳舞

把笑聲傳給星星
讓歌聲陪伴白浪跳舞
讓愛出聲
填飽生命每一個黑洞

大聲唱生日快樂
高聲唱新年快樂
祝你生日快樂
祝你新年快樂
因為別後
沉默長如海岸線
空白大如黑島天空

用我的方言
用你的方言
唱
祝你生日快樂
祝你新年快樂

聶魯達啊
甜甜的快樂
讓我們笑出鹹鹹的眼淚

2018.11

日出

日出前
火紅的光
燒山
像燃燒黑黑的大木炭
愈燒愈旺
冷卻後
留下
深深灼痛感

聶魯達啊
旭日視覺暫留
為什麼
停留這麼久
整片天空整片大地
都已成冷卻的黑木炭
我的眼目

我的腦海
還被一顆紅日強占

2018.11

愛情裡的祕密

你堅信
隱藏在愛情裡的祕密
啊，聶魯達
隱藏在愛情裡最大的祕密
是擁有祕密情人

你的摯愛
你用祕密詩篇突顯她
你用黑幕遮掩她

祕密的《船長詩篇》
是紙包不住火的祕密
你終於打開花苞
釋放玫瑰複瓣
愛情成為你人生的甜點
祕密成為你愛情的甜點

倘若
祕密成為永恆
結局會成為悲劇嗎？

2018.11

舌尖上

紅酒
在舌尖上
燙出許多張
泛紅臉譜

我的詩句
在舌尖上
酣暢
成長

聶魯達啊
我的愛
不在舌尖上
跳雙人舞步

我的愛
深藏心底

孤獨
孤獨唱歌
唱孤獨的歌

你將永遠聽不見孤獨
那歌詞
除非
你把耳朵朝向
我心深處

我的玫瑰

——在智利朗讀〈玫瑰物語〉

我挾帶玫瑰
走私南美
智利人看見我的玫瑰
閱讀我的玫瑰
我的玫瑰
狂飲葡萄園市金黃陽光
散發芳香
發出很多捲舌音的呢喃
從此擁有未完待續的玫瑰故事

我穿著玫瑰花瓣
羞澀走進你的黑島
聶魯達啊
我想把我的玫瑰
種在你的眼窩
你的耳洞
你的鼻腔

你的筆心你的深夢
我栽種我的玫瑰
在你的今朝你的明日
你的生生世世

在你用玫瑰紋身之前
玫瑰洗滌靈魂
用一千顆淚水

2018.11

天涯之國

飛渡萬里雲海
抵達天涯之國

一雙閃電的眼
追擊崖巔
一隻小山羊怯懦的心
太平洋沿岸傳播
海浪激情對話

是否冥冥中早有安排
詩人之國
連綿的岩山無際的大海
一再啟示我
更多靈感

在人生中途
你用詩照亮我的地圖

如果不是遇見你
此刻我會在哪裡
如果不是遇見你
我會朝聖哪一顆星

聶魯達啊
我欣喜
投向冥冥中的安排
文字是最初與最終的居所
誕生源源不絕幸福感

2018.11

光，籠罩我

聶魯達啊
我用謊言
塗了一臉大濃妝
在你眼神逼視中
紅妝一直一直掉
掉成落花

光，籠罩我
從頭髮到腳趾頭
我，花開
從外到裡
春天臨到

2018.11

時間在時鐘裡產生

時間在時鐘裡產生
陣痛
時鐘的長短針　遇合
時鐘的長短針　別離
我在時間裡　靜默
往事在時間裡　喋喋不休
我在靜默裡等待
醞釀花開
時間的長短針
如一把利剪
剪去憂傷剪斷歡笑

聶魯達啊
在你詩意的天空下
我的眼睛

一隻看到別離
一隻看見重逢

2018.11
《笠》329期，2019年2月

玫瑰與仙人掌

紅玫瑰
白仙人掌
同時眷愛你
聶魯達啊
你心中僅有的那把沃土
決定獻給哪一位

玫瑰
豔麗解語花
散放女人香
仙人掌
清麗脫俗害羞
把愛的花語埋藏心底

當你手捧仙人掌
你是不是悄悄思念玫瑰巧笑

當你擁抱玫瑰
你會不會偷偷心疼仙人掌

玫瑰有刺
仙人掌有刺
在兩者之間
你的手指會不會猶豫不決
兩朵奇葩
只能同時種進
無圍籬的詩篇

2018.11

仙人掌

遠避花花草草
仙人掌
在偏僻岩山荒地
尋獲自己的天堂

怕受傷
仙人掌學習刺蝟
穿戴戎裝
全面戒嚴
在陽光召喚下
開出純潔謙卑白花

同於玫瑰
仙人掌說
愛情
才是我的天堂

聶魯達啊
你準備好摘下這一朵
帶刺愛情花了嗎？

2018.11

仙人掌祈禱

仙人掌
向沒有一絲雲的天空祈禱
雨
不來就是不來

是不是
哭泣比祈禱容易
被神聽到
但仙人掌從古至今
都沒有學會哭泣
仙人掌只是堅持
早也祈禱
晚也祈禱
被我偷偷聽到

聶魯達啊
我在沒有你的季節祈禱你來

我學習用你的方言
晴天祈禱
雨天祈禱
你比上帝更難聽見
我喃喃跪禱

我學習仙人掌
持續不斷禱告
禱詞或許是一陣一陣風
會在某一瞬
忽然吹醒你耳朵

2018.11

荒山仙人掌

仙人掌
被逼退到邊陲
還是天性喜靜
自甘枯立偏僻荒山

仙人掌帶刺
不像一般花樹
擁有被春風玩弄
或玩弄春風的千百柔指

被蜂蝶遺忘
被雲雨遺忘
仙人掌有沒有自己的春天？

光明的季節
黑暗的季節
來來去去

荒山無悲無喜
仙人掌的念珠
是一顆一顆自閉的石頭

聶魯達啊
仙人掌開花時刻
你才驚覺
仙人掌不是石雕

2018.11

繁星

夜行
駱馬鎮*¹靜寂岩山
洛斯・維洛斯*²浪濤洶湧海岸
我一抬眼一舉步
都被繁星看見
我的獨白
全被繁星聽見
為了摘一朵玫瑰差點絆倒
也被繁星牢牢記住

想像繁星
是你微笑的眼睛
一眨眼飛濺出來的水晶碎片
黏貼在黑緞天幕
從此
我愛黑夜勝過白天

聶魯達啊

在這樣甜蜜無盡

夢幻無邊的藍夜

我蓋在暖被下的美夢

繁星再亮

也看不見

*[1]駱馬城：Vicuña，智利北方小鎮。
*[2]洛斯·維洛斯：Los Vilos，智利北方小鎮。

2018.11

詩牆

面對一面牆
凝思
各國詩人一筆一劃寫下詩句
像品種不同藤蔓
攀緣牆壁

為了不和別人藤蔓糾纏
我小心翼翼
壓抑藤蔓慾望
控制藤蔓肢體延展方向

為了讓你
直達我心
我捨棄熟悉的象形文字
讓藤蔓蔓延西班牙語莖葉：
　　我迷失
　　在你語言曲折的迷宮

聶魯達啊

你認真研讀的眼睛是春陽

促使藤蔓開花

你讚歎的舌尖掀起春風

促使藤蔓舞蹈

你憐憫的心長出一株曼妙藤蔓

與我的藤蔓

陽光中交纏

交纏

2018.11
《笠》329期，2019年2月

朗讀金屬性的笑聲

南美詩人朗讀金屬性的笑聲*1
台灣詩人朗讀金屬性的笑聲
男詩人朗讀金屬性的笑聲
女詩人朗讀金屬性的笑聲

笑聲誘發笑聲
像面對山谷告白
引發甜蜜迴響

聶魯達啊
你像感冒失聲的詩人*2
但我從智利人的嘴型
聽到你的笑聲
看見你的笑臉

智利人
時常用笑聲和我交談

笑聲使得眼睛

那兩條發呆

嗜睡的魚

有了逆游而上的神力

笑聲是一把金鑰匙

打開天堂密門

*[1] 〈金屬性的笑聲〉，詩人李魁賢《給智利的情詩20首》第6首。
*[2] 台灣詩人李魁賢在詩會期間感冒失聲，只能由陳秀珍代讀華語部分，西班牙語一律由薩爾瓦多詩人Oscar René Benítez朗讀。

2018.11

愛

懷孕
愛
是美好的
請勿用你雙手
你的雙唇
催生我的愛

懷孕
曖昧的愛
是幸福的
請勿用你耳語
你的咒語
接生我的愛

懷孕
愛
像一場不想醒來

醒不過來的美夢
愛的指痕腳印蓋在肚腹
再也藏不住

聶魯達啊
難產的愛
陣痛的愛
使人深刻感覺愛
存在

2018.11

你將把我送往何處

夕陽謝幕
晚雲橫貫天際
像一條白色緞帶
把世界包裝成為精美禮物

旅途勞頓
人藏在世界深處
塞進車廂打盹
心緒一路起伏
被路過的山月看見

時間奔馳
和夜車比賽速度
從來不知疲睏
時間啊時間
將把我送往何處？
送給誰當禮物？

時間滴答滴答
心跳不止
啊，聶魯達
我聽見你磁性男聲
一貫溫柔回答：
時間
站在愛情這一邊

2018.11
《笠》329期，2019年2月

我害怕

一朵粉紅微笑
使玫瑰失色

你微笑
你不微笑
你的眼波
都泛起
被女巫偷吻的漣漪

我是玫瑰
愛你微笑
我是女巫
愛你眼波掀起溫柔

不
我不愛你微笑
不愛你眼波

你的微笑你的眼波
是錯誤路標
使我在坦直大道急轉彎

聶魯達啊
祕徑給予我夢幻雲霧
我好期待
我好害怕
我不熟悉的山徑
躲藏猛獅

2018.11

那一天

那一天
我很想潛入海底躲藏
很想飛入雲翼隱藏
你捉住我的腳
折斷我翅膀

那一天
走在曾經海嘯的海邊
寒風像猛獸
我逆風詳閱沙灘
想要揀拾一枚
填滿大海歌聲的貝殼
紀念我在天涯遇見你的歷史
沙灘精心的收藏
像一句句誓言
早已落入許多情侶口袋

聶魯達啊
我害怕
那一天會像那枚貝殼
埋進時間的萬千沙粒中
使我翻尋不到

2018.11

寒

初春深宵
套上層層冬衣
像一顆洋蔥
埋進黑壤的厚被
等待旭日
讓我發芽

聶魯達啊
在我萌芽之前
快快快快伸出厚實雙手
我想握住
一個暖春

黑島冰冷海水
顫抖等待
如火太陽

沸騰
愛

2018.11

前進駱馬城

以車代馬
前進駱馬城
四圍岩山裸裎真面目
近處才有綠樹衝破地牢
太陽把岩山當成實驗畫布
隨晨昏轉換用色

翻過多少山頭
不見鳥蹤未聞鳥鳴
詩人*為我指出谷間藍湖
湖被群山折彎
時隱
時現

翻越多少念頭
或許也翻過
山楂或角豆樹

杏花或無花果林
黃昏岩山轉透明淡紫
終於來到駱馬城

聶魯達啊
我不成為流不到海的那湖
不成為只會發呆的樹
越過多少寂寞落日
總算來到詩人之國
若你是岩山
我就化成種籽
種進你身體
成為你的骨

*指智利詩人Luis Sepulveda Castro

2018.11

你的愛

你的愛
何其飄渺
真實的時候
短暫停留我手上
像候鳥
拔給我幾片羽毛
讓我獨自抵抗漫漫嚴冬

你的愛
何其溫柔
甜美
你用有體溫的文字
跨越山海穿越時空
緊緊擁抱我

你的愛
何其廣大

充塞我身體
我生存的宇宙
我呼吸你的愛
無時無刻

你的愛
何其神妙
在我看不到你的時候
體會你存在
在我聽不見你的時候
我心跳如鼓動
繼續往前向你朝聖

你的愛
何其殘酷
在我決心抗拒愛你時
你突然現身

我閉不上轉不開
脆弱的眼睛

你的愛
何其仁慈
在我因你而受傷
而生病時
成為我唯一靈藥

聶魯達啊
伸出你神聖雙手
為尚未痊癒的我施洗
我祈求成為
你唯一的聖徒

2018.11
《笠》329期，2019年2月

我的虔誠

聶魯達啊
我用你的文字編成魔巾
摺疊自己的心意
我用你的文字織成手絹
擦拭我的淚我的血
我用你的文字堆疊雲山
禪坐
我用你的文字築成修道院
閉門苦修
我用你的文字鋪成道路
三跪九叩

匍匐
在冷漠天空下
我親吻有時太冰
有時發燙的大地
像親吻你的腳趾

你溫柔的文字

不知何故變成石塊

磨破我膝蓋

我額頭叩出黑色死皮

我忍痛

繼續三跪九叩

叩昏天與地

因為你在前方

你就在前方

你在遙遠遙遠彼岸

隱約

對我聲聲傳喚

2018.11

戀愛事件

極光
在暗黑天空
燃放綠色煙火
沒有星星看見
沒有人見證
沒有眼睛的天空
看不見

小花
從大樹監牢
死命鑽出
沒有夜鶯看見小花偷笑
沒有蝴蝶聞到小花送香
沒有耳朵的大樹
聽不見花
開的聲音

魚夫
釣鉤鉤滿愛情靈糧
垂進飢餓的河水
浮雲飄行水面
一朵、兩朵、三朵……
沒有一隻魚眼看見

聶魯達啊
風一陣又一陣
飄逝
好像戀愛
從來不曾發生

2018.11

夢

夢是一隻小獸
擁有美色
與玫瑰一般受寵

我擁抱他
親吻他
我愛撫他
我餵食他整夜星空
他是我唯一寵物

夢
嚼食星星
一顆、兩顆、三顆……
他開始擁有你
星光閃爍的眼睛

聶魯達啊

他眼睛燃放光芒

我開始清楚看見

他擁有你玫瑰紅唇

像夜色的柔髮

最重要

他的手學會你的句法

我發誓

他是以文字為武器

最厲害的詩人

有時

他惡作劇藏身密林

讓越來越目盲的我

心急

聶魯達啊
夢的獠牙嚼完整夜星空
轉頭嚼食
亞當捨給我的肋骨
使我有說不出的
痛

2018.11

你是

你是星光
在黑色星星的長夜
我從心掏出泛黃
和新鮮如檸檬汁的詩句
因為知道
星星會再度點亮
潑墨的夜

你是一座山
栽種出紅的黃的白的
膚色玫瑰
也有憂傷的荊棘
總會有風把我吹向山
沒人理解
我來看紅葉凋盡的楓樹
卻不絕望

因為確信
冬雪過後春草將掙出黑土

你是一座海洋
擁有立體主義多變面向
你的語言掀起浪潮
萬千崇拜你的魚
優游成為逗點
我祈求成為一座海洋
我要伸出千萬隻浪花的手
將成為小魚的你
溫柔覆蓋
覆蓋
在我深不可測的神祕漩渦

2018.11

慕光1

叢林
閃現螢光
我看見溫暖
將擴散的希望之光

我邁開腳步
追尋光點集結的山坡
微弱光點忽然被千千萬萬
逆光的手追緝
向光的眼睛
被千千萬萬不義之手
追緝

在這一頁
歷史上的螢光熄滅
我眼睛的光熄滅

聶魯達啊
宇宙如此黑暗
我試圖把手
伸進你的詩篇
捕捉
幸福螢光
你會為我平反嗎？

2018.11.25
《笠》329期，2019年2月

慕光2

「面對黑暗
你要成為螢光」
這是每一隻螢火蟲
想要留給慕光者
唯一的遺言

面對黑暗
有人熄滅心中火種
變成黑暗的牆

聶魯達啊
你在安穩的生活中
西班牙在你心中*
你是一點螢光
對抗巨大黑暗
在你螢光中
我思考

如何成為一隻螢火蟲
台灣在我心中

恍惚
聽見螢的先知
啟示：
探索螢的心路
繼承螢的心事
無退路

在黑暗背景中
我漸漸分辨出
誰是螢光
照亮黑牆

*《西班牙在我心中》，聶魯達的作品。

2018.11.25
《笠》329期2019.2月號

不一樣的我

洗滌千萬次
手留有
洗也洗不淡的花香

歷經季節霜寒
身體牢牢記住
那熾夏溫度

眼睛
穿越落葉雨雪
無數落日
直抵那最甜蜜的時光

耳朵
反覆重播
一成不變的聲音
我終於學會獨唱

你的情歌
忘記世上
還有許許多多旋律

聶魯達啊
世界喑啞時
世界爭吵時
我唱你
教給我的那一首詩歌
唱到紅玫瑰
盛開全宇宙

2018.11

如果

如果你贈我耳環
我會想到
天神用弦月金鉤
垂釣整夜星空

如果你送我指環
我會想像
童話中
最小的甜甜圈
最難擺脫的小手銬

如果你送我鮮花
我會想像
一株薔薇開在你庭院
花香
是我寫給你的詩

聶魯達啊
就算你送我全世界
都不及你
一個推不開的擁抱
如果你向我索求禮物
我一無所有
除了
一顆過敏的心

2018.11

棉被

棉被
孵化萬里星空
每顆星替代老綿羊
一顆星星，兩顆星星，三顆星星……
每顆星化為文字
替代你的詩
催眠
催眠

星空下
大地板塊擠壓
使我位移
但我始終學不會
讀懂斑駁星圖

棉被
解讀主人夢

全盤了解主人心事
給予主人需求的溫度

聶魯達啊
你在太平洋另一岸
黑島春天星空閃爍
你不了解棉被寂寞

2018.11

殘酷戀人

夜空大監獄
囚禁月亮的孩子
滿天星星眨動天真眼睛
顯然樂當女囚

花園集中營
關押樹和草的孩子
花朵顯然很情願
各自化上豔彩濃妝
向人向神爭寵

海岸圍牆
迫使浪花無從上岸
但浪花日夜與岸
打拍子合唱

聶魯達啊
戀人攜手走過
如此殘酷風景
心裡毫無
一絲憐憫

2018.11

在愛裡

四目遙望
經過的紫山
聽見仙人掌
祈禱開花的謙卑願望

幸福囚徒
一再鎖進車廂
海浪不倦
拍擊黑岩白岩琴鍵

聶魯達啊
寫絕世情詩的手
用文字革命的手
要改變國家命運
卻無意中改變我命運的手

像騎士
你擁抱我
擁抱中感受無盡憂傷
河將流向自己的海洋
雲將飄回自己的山坳

憂傷中
感覺愛
存在
在愛中學習星星
發出光芒

聖誕禮物

聖誕老公公
背一個大紅袋
裝滿祝福的禮物
乘雪橇穿過漫天風雪
鈴聲中從煙管溜下來

時間滴答滴答
像心跳
我怕等太久會睡著

現代聖誕老公公
從網路竄出來
他的大紅包袋
鼓著滿滿一句話
我讓你讓妳發大財

人們不再花時間
打扮聖誕樹
不再癡癡等待
蝴蝶打結的禮物
紅包會從天空掉下來
比雨季雨點多更多
比櫻花祭落英多更多

發了大財
可以買萬隻襪子裝禮物
誰在乎聖誕節
誰在乎
慢吞吞的聖誕老人

聖誕老人腳步聲
時近時遠
聶魯達啊

我耐心守候寒夜
你是我向上帝
日夜跪求的聖誕禮物

2018.11.30
《笠》329期2019.2月號

米斯特拉爾故居

在米斯特拉爾簡陋的故居
想像文學巨人
少小模樣與生活景況

偏僻深山
駱馬城鄉親無法想像
山中貧困女孩
日後摘下諾貝爾文學獎
好像不比摘下一顆檸檬困難

庭前樹
層層疊疊岩山
無言的天空
淳樸熱情山民
背叛的情人自殺身亡……
米斯特拉爾啊

妳人生劇情似駱馬城這山路
曲折

愛情
比諾貝爾文學獎更難獲得
妳在死亡的十四行*
淌下熱淚多少行
我偷偷為妳拭去憂傷
妳的淚濕了
我的心

*《死亡十四行》，米斯特拉爾為自殺身亡的情人而寫的詩。

2018.11.29

在米斯特拉爾紀念館

相片、詩集、文物⋯⋯
專屬過米斯特拉爾
如今變成世人共享的資產

即使文字形成隔閡
影像褪色
還是可以捕捉到
舊時代的光與影

窗口
米斯特拉爾半身雕像
面對一張小孩大合照
突顯她教師形象
我坐她身旁抬頭仰望
感受沉鬱雕像
釋放無比能量

駱馬城春風撫過
窗口
她的臉
我的臉

我把米斯特拉爾
裝進心裡帶回台北
雕像留給駱馬城

2018.11.29

夢境

——致文森·維多夫羅[1]

你我之間
隔著一層薄土
不
是隔著一層睡眠
或者是一個夢

我被困
在門外
千把鑰匙打不開
你說：用詩打開千扇門

聽見落葉
還在你詩中飄落
飛舞
我內心震動不已

丟掉沒有生命的形容詞*²
歌頌夜鶯
讓夜鶯在詩的密林展喉歌唱
歌頌蜜蜂
讓蜂蜜從文字滑落

詩人
你是一位小小上帝*³
我願
活在你的創世紀

*¹文森‧維多夫羅（Vicente Huidobro ,1893~1948），創造主義
　（Creacionismo）倡議者。
*²文森‧維多夫羅詩〈詩藝〉中主張拋棄形容詞。
*³文森‧維多夫羅詩〈詩藝〉結句：「詩人是一位小小上帝」。

2018.11

我將玫瑰獻上

——致奧斯卡‧卡斯特羅

我手持一支紅玫瑰
你活在火豔豔的玫瑰

再強的風
颳不走你的禱詞
你的詩被譜成曲*
智利大街小巷傳唱
你的浪漫

在月下在百合花香中
你的孤獨
確確實實親吻了
我的孤獨
我將玫瑰獻上
陪伴你
深深的睡眠

你心靈噙著擦不乾的淚水
我怎能遺忘你
你的名字是詩人
奧斯卡·卡斯特羅

*奧斯卡·卡斯特羅的詩〈祈禱勿忘我〉等。

2018.11

幻想曲1

眼睛的魚
在臉的小島
游啊游
游不到
鼻梁隆起的山
眼淚直直掉

聶魯達啊
距離如此短
思念如此漫長

幻想曲2

誰
提著一盞夕陽燈籠
往山坳
往海底
尋找迷路星星

聶魯達啊
星星不曾消逝
只是變成天藍色
想要看見
你思思念念

幻想曲3

滿天星星
在夜的道場集體靜坐
冥想
冥想冥想
變成月亮
變成太陽

聶魯達啊
你在我心
祕密道場靜坐冥想
冥想
冥想……

思路

一字一字
鋪成一條思路
我在字裡佇立
在句裡流連
在詩篇裡安居
尋找生命意義

我藏在字句間
屏息
聽你呼吸心跳
感受你
喜悅如鷗鳥
憂傷似黑礁

在你我之間
用詩一字一字
引渡

每一首詩統一嘴型
呼喚同一個名
聶魯達啊
聶魯達

智利春草

不想被當無用雜草
在雜草間
掙出鮮花

不想被囚進花瓶
拚命從花轉型
成為蒴果
儲滿生命蜜汁

甜蜜
從果到花
香味
從花到枝與葉

我這般努力
讓你看見我的努力

聶魯達啊
你眸光有沒有轉向我

當你定睛
在我身上
我已不再只是果實

2018.12

過境

海浪、防風林
…………
沒有主角的風景

荒地等候春天
不休不眠
等到春天
臉紅心跳

廢棄鐵道
等不到火車
我在此等待你
是我
還是你遲到？

聶魯達啊
春天終將被夏風吹走

時鐘催逼日曆
日曆催逼戀情
我把耳朵貼近隱隱鼓聲
努力
不使黑髮變白

2018.12

聶魯達啊

聶魯達啊
你擋住我的鐘面
使我看不清
歲月的臉
每一小時
你都報錯時間

聶魯達啊
你取代我的鏡面
使我分不清
你的臉我的臉
每分每秒用微笑補妝
你的臉
就是我的容顏

聶魯達啊
你用舌堵住我的口

小小世界裡
不再有黑白是非
你的唇替代我的心
發聲

2018.12

你怎能

你把手臂圈成
一座港灣
一條項鍊
一副手銬

春天
張開豔陽口舌
吸吮我
全身水分

聶魯達啊
你怎能
在我眼中縱火
淚水再多
澆不熄
焚身烈焰

2018.12

薄紫

黃昏
岩山薄紫透明
我長出幻想的翅膀

月下
我飛進你眼穴
營巢

午夜
我被風吹進你的夢歷險
明明你掛起弓與箭
我卻遍體鱗傷

聶魯達啊
不勞而獲的獵人
我須在你靈魂深處
療傷

2019.01.01

緝毒

入境智利
值勤的狗滿臉正義
圍繞我行李
嗅了又嗅
難道
他的肺葉偏好我的香水

出境智利
緝毒的狗
滿臉嚴肅鼻孔專注
糾纏我的行李
聞了又聞
若有所思

面對官方嚴厲盤查
聶魯達啊
我內心忐忑不安

我的行李確確實實
偷渡一個吻

2019.01

【附錄】循詩人軌跡，遇見聶魯達
——2018第14屆智利【詩人軌跡】國際詩歌節
紀要（Tras las Huellas del Poeta 10.17~10.28）

循【詩人軌跡】前行

聶魯達的智利、米斯特拉爾的智利、奧斯卡·卡斯特羅的智利、文森·維多夫羅的智利、切·格瓦拉老舊摩托車穿行過的智利……

10月16日，台灣即將入冬，我攜帶10本漢英西三語詩集《保證》，跟隨攜帶20本《給智利的情詩20首》的李魁賢老師飛往智利之春，為實踐他念茲在茲的「台灣意象，文學先行」，我們再次自囚於宛如流動監獄的飛機。不包括洛杉磯與達拉斯冗長轉機，從桃園飛抵聖地亞哥大約24.5小時。

天涯之國

智利共和國（República de Chile）與阿根廷及巴西並列南美ABC強國。國土南北狹長如絲帶，智利人常稱自己國家為「天涯之國」。西和南瀕臨太平洋，北接祕魯，東鄰玻利維亞和阿根廷，位於美洲大陸最南，與南極洲隔海相望。接壤祕魯的北部在西班牙入侵前是印加帝國一部分。幾乎終年不雨、地球最乾燥的阿他加馬沙漠，在安地斯山脈兩條山脊間。智利近年吸引亞裔與鄰國移居，我們曾親見移民機關一早就排了申請移民的人龍。

2018年智利【詩人軌跡】

參加詩人有台灣：李魁賢、陳秀珍；智利：Luis Arias Manzo；薩爾瓦多：Oscar René Benítez；哥倫比亞：Maggy Gomez Sepulveda、Jose Rolando Bedoya Avalos；阿根廷：Susana Goldemberg；墨西哥：Arcelia Cruces de Axipuru、Lorena Aixpuru；智利：各地參加者數十位。

期程長達12天，走訪聶魯達（Pablo Neruda）三處故居；米斯特拉爾（Gabriela Mistral）故居、墓園與紀念館；詩人作家奧斯卡·卡斯特羅（Oscar Mistral）墓園與基金會；文森·維多夫羅（Vicente Huidobro）墓園。

另一重點是與各地各級學校、圖書館、文化中心交流。從首都到偏遠山村，智利師生熱情活潑、誠懇貼心、踴躍發問，擁有自由不羈的拉美靈魂。

10.17（三）第1天：聖地亞哥

晨07:48抵達智利首都聖地亞哥，與晚2小時抵達的薩爾瓦多詩人，也是PPdM美洲區副會長的Oscar，一起被PPdM創辦人Luis Arias

Manzo接到Hotel Carlton。途中我認真觀賞風景與路況，想要把聖地亞哥看進深心。春天首都，許多行道樹盛開白花，淡雅迷人；紫花次多，增添首都浪漫氣息；紅色是搶眼的配角。路況平整暢通。

下午到附近學校（Valentin Letelier）交流。我隨身攜帶三語詩集《保證》（李老師策劃的【台灣詩叢】，秀威出版，李魁賢英譯，簡瑞玲西譯）。我朗讀〈讀詩〉，Oscar為我讀西語版。學生相當投入，老師也熱情提問。詩人被詢及寫詩動機。我的〈讀詩〉，寫2015年台南福爾摩莎國際詩歌節，最後一夜在日月潭最後一場朗讀的心情，未料當時同場朗讀者竟有五人在此重逢，並再度同台朗詩，心中感慨係之！朗詩時，台下女學生信筆為我素描人像。

17:00參觀聶魯達聖地亞哥故居La Chascona博物館。聶魯達（Pablo Neruda,1904-1973）1971年以《情詩・哀詩・贊詩》獲諾貝爾文學獎，理由：詩歌具有自然力般的作用，復甦了一個大陸的命運與夢想。

La Chascona，聶魯達1951年為祕密情人所購，彼時他與第二任妻子德里婭・德爾卡里爾（Delia del Carril）尚存婚姻關係。La Chascona，意謂瑪蒂爾德・伍魯蒂亞（Matilde Urrutia）狂亂的頭髮。

參訪者只許由屋外往內拍照，不得在室內拍藏品，加以時間有限，我只能走馬看花，留下琳瑯滿目印象。

明淨落地窗，透進溫暖日照。風格迥異藏品，十分搭調毫無違和感。像小型骨董博物館，館長具有致命戀物及收藏癖。樓梯窄仄，只容一人迴旋，每一室雖不大，但綜觀整體建築群落，規模不小，庭園花木宜人，想必也會引來蟲鳴鳥叫、天光雲影徘徊。

　　藏品洩漏藏家品味、嗜好、祕密，置身此夢幻空間，我看到聶魯達愛海成痴，海的意象無所不在。進行收藏像經營一首情詩，象徵意義的物件、給愛人的私密訊息、護身符、火烈鳥標本、非洲木雕、與實物等比例的銅馬、50倍大的男鞋……。感官主義的浪漫靈魂，讓物件在房間各角落細訴私密故事，訪者各自心中解讀。我想像，聶魯達即將從一扇特殊祕門現身，戴著面具……。

　　一張長木桌幾乎占盡餐廳，桌面擺放瓷器、玻璃器皿，以及精美盤碟。不經意撞見的眼睛吊飾在樹幹、在杯面、在庭院，我竟有處處被監看的不安！

　　步出La Chascona，沿下坡道，近距離看到正當花季的白花樹，很想問人樹名。陽光送暖，空氣乾爽，呼吸舒暢，腳步變輕快。

　　迎賓晚宴，各國詩人盛裝赴會，詩人李魁賢與我被安排在主賓座。眾多詩人被一一介紹後，大都還來不及交談認識，即宴盡人散。

　　夜間，裹羊駝毛外套著厚襪，躲進層被，寒意不盡，絲毫不像台灣春天！但即便全世界都風雪，我小小心房始終點燃一把火焰，照亮聶魯達的臉。

10.18（四）第2天：蘭卡瓜（Rancagua）→聖地亞哥

　　晨，驅車至蘭卡瓜（Rancagua），浪漫派詩人奧斯卡·卡斯特羅（Oscar Castro,1910-1947）墓園。

　　詩人專車方抵墓園，奧斯卡·卡斯特羅之孫Miguel Alcaya

Castro，亦即奧斯卡·卡斯特羅基金會總裁（Presidente Fundacion Oscar Enrique Castro Zuñiga），已在入口處迎賓。以朝聖之心，詩人人手一枝紅豔康乃馨齊步走向奧斯卡·卡斯特羅墓地獻花、念詩。我藉康乃馨向浪漫詩人傾訴：熱烈愛你！

奧斯卡·卡斯特羅名作〈祈禱勿忘我〉，被譜曲傳唱智利大街小巷。在墓園，音樂家暨詩人Sergio Teran Cortez以吉他伴奏詩人合唱。李魁賢老師除了獻詩給奧斯卡·卡斯特羅，更贈其孫《給智利的情詩20首》。

走一段路，經過不喧囂的街區，到成人高中Francisco Tello朗讀。

中午在蘭卡瓜一家餐廳用膳。像演說家的廚師，席前說了一堆話，詩人都洗耳恭聽。台灣好像行行皆繁忙，沒人有耐性說話，更遑論耐心聽人說話。我所行經的蘭卡瓜純樸可愛，因奧斯卡·卡斯特羅而馳名。

餐後詩人與藝術家彈吉他合唱，處處流洩隨性、浪漫族性！餐廳提供一面蛋黃色牆面給詩人揮灑。我在兩屆淡水福爾摩莎國際詩歌節寫過玻璃詩，寫牆詩卻是平生第一遭。牆與玻璃一樣，垂直運筆困難！

下午參訪奧斯卡·卡斯特羅基金會，經導覽、影片、現代劇場、座談，進一步認識這位作家，驚訝得知，由於風流倜儻，尚留有不知名姓子孫流落在外。

晚餐在the old Wall（Rancagua）。除了人，四圍幾乎皆骨董，懷舊風輕輕吹。下午與學校交流，我朗讀了〈曼陀羅2〉，因而與智利女詩人暨藝術家Elina Torres Verdugo打開話匣，她用手機螢幕展示她設計的曼陀羅圖案。席間，年邁老闆中氣十足唱歌娛賓，Luis Arias Manzo與Maggy Gomez Sepulveda聞樂相擁起舞。一女扮男裝歌手壓軸演唱纏綿情歌，對席中男詩人，尤其是Oscar投懷送抱，極盡挑逗。今年淡水詩歌節在忠寮有相似劇情。

10.19（五）第3天：Huechuraba圖書館→梅里匹拉（Melipilla）

09:30國際詩人抵達韋丘拉瓦（Huechuraba）鎮圖書館文字管理局，會場群書環繞，與會人潮擠爆。我與人群一一擁抱、貼臉、問候，一天之始，有愛同行。南美人善用肢體建立溫暖人際關係，我極羨慕並享受如此溫馨傳遞，很懷疑我體內流有南美人血液。

每位詩人都接受到一面小小紙國旗。館方特地安排一位年輕譯者給台灣詩人，所以每當西語朗詩時，都請其代勞。熱情的他，也表達對台灣的好奇與興趣。

參訪兩校，第一所學校聖瑪爾塔（Escuela Santa Marta），幼稚園學生毫無怯意表演舞蹈，成人表演智利國舞奎卡舞（cueca）以及歌唱；國際詩人則朗詩回饋。第二所學校，會場牆壁掛滿師生的手工織品，學生也朗讀他們的詩作。詩人之國，生活就是詩！

午餐在Villa Moreira，人多，氣氛熱絡。

參訪兩校及兩古蹟後，重返圖書館受獎，獎品是一瓶智利紅酒，驚喜！

往北移居山區梅里匹拉（Melipilla）旅館。溫暖舒適。

燭光晚宴時，墨西哥優雅女詩人Arcelia Cruces de Axipuru偕親切的女兒Lorena Aixpuru從機場趕來加入詩歌節行列。

10.20（六）第4天：瓦爾帕萊索（Valparaiso）

上午9點從梅里匹拉出發，前往聶魯達瓦爾帕萊索故居La Sebastiana博物館。車程漫漫，一路鄉野風光。山大都草木疏短，白楊以玉樹臨風之姿搶鏡頭。偶有羊、馬點綴草原。6月在非洲，為其夏日繁花讚歎；如今智利春天，野花狂野浪漫，不遑多讓！最大宗橘黃花，織成連綿花毯，智利之春最經典彩妝。

通過一個驚險大斜坡，才駛抵La Sebastiana。

瓦爾帕萊索（Valparaiso）意為天堂谷。La Sebastiana築於佛羅里達山坡，1959年購自建築師塞巴斯蒂安·科利亞（Sebastián Collado），房屋以其名命名。五層樓，仍以大面積落地窗溝通內外部空間，透過明淨玻璃窗，房室內臟一覽無遺。油畫、馬賽克木桌、木馬、家具等繁複瑰麗。窄樓梯、矮門與低天花板，感覺好像緩行在一艘船上，行經樓板時腳下發出吱嘎吱嘎聲。完全被吧台占據的房間，餐桌擺放目不暇給的彩色玻璃杯，聶魯達晚年買的一隻綿羊玩具，彌補幾十年前丟失的心愛玩具。寫作室桌旁一個水槽，方便寫作前洗手習慣。晨光中他寫作，午後外出會友。

關於玩心，聶魯達自述：我收集許多玩具，沒有玩具我活不下去，不玩的孩子不算是孩子，不玩的大人將永遠失喪活在心中的童心，像造玩具那般我建造我的房子，並在其中從早玩到晚。

不同面向窗戶，或鳥瞰港口，或遠眺山坡層層疊疊彩屋。二度來訪的李魁賢老師，再度以九十度彎腰姿勢，極有耐性在留言簿上用漢英雙語題字：「第二次來參觀，繼2014年第一次後，印象仍然深刻！Still very impressive at this second visit after first one in 2014.」前院以聶魯達側影打造的座椅，成為遊客搶合照的景點。附近詩人廣場，有維多夫羅、米斯特拉爾坐姿銅像，與站立迎送晨昏的聶魯達銅像。

在瓦爾帕萊索一個險峻大斜坡上，有條爭奇鬥豔的塗鴉街，具現拉美人熱情奔放心性，過目難忘。

下午到比尼亞德爾馬（Liceo Bicentenario Viña）與當地詩人和作家交流，座無虛席。我朗讀〈玫瑰物語〉，主持的詩人José Miguel Torres為我朗讀西語版。詩人與聽眾會及時發出共鳴，氣氛熱絡。

大約下午4點返回旅館，休息至19:00乘車至附近梅里匹拉文化中心（the Cultural Center Edetrem of Melipilla）。

踏入會場，撞見與真人同比例詩人肖像海報，一排年輕吉他手靠牆而坐。吉他浪漫開場，詩人一一上台朗讀。詩樂交響，紅酒、西點，是詩人的晚餐。

10.21（日）第5天：黑島（Isla Negra）→卡塔赫納（Cartagena）

房間窗戶朝東，晨起觀日，旭日從遠山躍出速度極快，與北非慢吞吞日出極不同，巨星出場還是要吊足觀眾胃口較好！

9點前往聶魯達故居黑島（Isla Negra）。在「黑島之家」舉辦國際詩人新書發表會。詩人李魁賢首先發表與Luis合編的漢英西三語版詩集《兩半球詩路》第二集，由詩人Oscar René Benitez幫忙口譯。

黑島並非島嶼，臨太平洋，位於岩石遍布、濤聲激昂的海岸線上，是大詩人三居所中最讓我驚豔的一處。豔陽下，海濱岩石中黃、紅、白、橘、紫……繁花姿影，日後屢屢隨風搖曳入夢；激情浪濤，時時翻騰心中。這般場景最宜演繹不朽詩情：「我渴望你的雙唇，你的聲音，你的頭髮。安靜而饑渴地，我遊盪街頭。麵包滋養不了我，黎明讓我分裂，一整天我搜尋你兩腳流動的聲響。」

在此，海洋主題更加顯豁。航海設備霸占客廳，牆上十數裝飾船頭的女神像。這些船頭雕飾是聶魯達最大的玩具。不可或缺的餐櫃和大餐桌、大壁爐與椅子。臥室編織精細的白色蕾絲床單散發浪漫氣息。即使步出室外，我腦海還泊滿瓶中船。聶魯達沉迷瓶中船，每艘都有來歷，都用文字載明船名、桅杆、船帆、船頭和錨。不屬於玩具的一面諾貝爾文學獎牌在此閃耀。

有一室，專藏形形色色珍稀貝殼。海螺是聶魯達平生最精美的收藏，他說：海螺奇妙的結構，月光般皎潔的細瓷，加以具有厚實感的、哥德式的實用外殼。

室外有聶魯達與伍魯蒂雅永眠之所，不仔細看，會把極簡墓地當花圃。墓碑，右刻Pablo Neruda,1904-1973，左刻Matilde Urrutia,1912-1985。

　　藍海、白浪、礁岩、繁花、綠樹……黑島海岸景觀如此多樣。豔陽讓我睜不開眼，但海風實在強勁，我抱胸不住發抖。面對錄影機我們輪流用各自的語言唱生日快樂歌，後來才知是要送給PPdM駐洛斯·維洛斯領事David Altamirano Hernandez。

　　1973年9月，右派軍頭皮諾契特（Augusto Pinochet）發動政變，推翻聶魯達社會主義盟友薩爾瓦多·阿連德（Salvador Allende）政府，阿連德在政變當天身亡。不久後，聶魯達在醫院過世。從此，伍魯蒂雅返回聖地亞哥La Chascona度過餘生。

　　文森·維多夫羅（Vicente Huidobro，1893-1948）永眠之地卡塔赫納（Cartagena）山坡，距黑島不遠。維多夫羅生於聖地亞哥富家。1911年，出版〈Ecos del alma〉（靈魂的迴聲），具現代主義色彩。1916年赴歐，在巴黎與前衛藝術家談詩論藝，成為前衛詩人，開創了創造主義（Creacionismo）。

　　聶魯達批評維多夫羅醉心於法國的時新式樣，進而改造此式樣，使其適合他的生存和表達方式。他認為維多夫羅已超越了自己的模本。

　　面對山景麗日，維多夫羅墓園確是福地。前衛詩人選擇直立入葬，國際詩人在此朗詩致敬。

　　晚餐於梅里匹拉。宿梅里匹拉第三夜，翌日將移居。明顯感受天氣趨暖和。

10.22（一）第6天：梅里匹拉（Melipilla）→洛斯‧維洛斯（Los Vilos）

10點在梅里匹拉參訪文化館（Culture House: Teatro Ignacio Serrano）以及社區。天氣乾爽舒暢，狗懶洋洋躺在公園曬太陽。這個小鎮不慌不忙。

11點參訪梅里匹拉的學校（the College Republic of Brazil in Melipilla）。朗詩後，我被點名接受考問：屬於哪種詩風、第一首詩寫於何時、幾歲……等等。小學生的問題格外生猛有趣，面對炯炯發亮眼睛，我絞盡腦汁回答，卻難周全。純真熱情小孩自動要求合照，童心就是詩！

藍布巾手繪各種花卉，從小物件看見生活美好質感。中餐，學校招待烤厚餡薄餅，餡料有蛋、洋蔥、雞胸肉、橄欖……爆汁的智利美食滿足台灣胃，回味無窮，最難忘的一餐！

下午長征至洛斯‧維洛斯（Los Vilos）。從比尼亞德爾馬（Liceo Bicentenario Viña）往洛斯‧維洛斯，沿途地貌多變，綺麗蒼勁兼具。左邊是時近時遠波濤洶湧的海洋，經過一段奇詭礁岩，變成沙岸，接著又是荒涼沙丘，有時換成低谷丘陵；右邊是丘陵、岩山、河流、沼澤、草原，處處黃橘野花，時而夾雜紫白紅，山壁則成為野花花牆，空闊草原偶現馬羊。

抵達洛斯‧維洛斯民宿，熱情愛搞笑的David已等在車門外，我與他是初識，但早已在黑島錄影唱生日快樂祝福他了。此後媒體採訪報導就全靠他了。

　　一下車我奔進只容一張單人床的海邊小屋，套上羊駝外套與手套。原以為好天氣會蔓延到這裡！趁晚餐前空檔跟隨詩人李魁賢、Oscar René Benítez、Jose Rolando Bedoya Avalos、Arcelia Cruces de Axipuru、Lorena Aixpuru去看夕陽。六人沿小鎮邊緣散步，聽說這是窮鄉。沿途商店古樸，欠缺輝煌燈火與明亮玻璃窗。以一個過客的嗅覺，我並未聞到絲毫窮酸味，反倒看見許多懷舊的光影。整條路上沒有匆促急躁腳步，我多麼享受這裡的氣氛，希望可以無盡漫步。緩坡上這城鎮，似乎越走越寬闊。

　　轉進下坡巷道，通往海岸，但這方向看不到日落。海浪澎湃中聽聞此處曾發生海嘯。海風冰冷，但晚霞與漸漸燃起的遠方燈火，使這素樸海岸變得詩意盎然。

　　海濱小屋以其狹隘又寒氣逼人令我難忘。

10.23（二）第7天：洛斯‧維洛斯（Los Vilos）

　　上午參訪位於海邊的洛斯‧維洛斯文化中心。此地有長毛象遺跡，一萬兩千年前就有原住民。古蹟活化的文化中心，曾作聶魯達等大師紀念展。另外，蜥蜴、甲蟲……標本亦令我印象深刻。

　　下一站到電台受訪，由李魁賢老師英譯，Oscar西譯。被問1.妳對洛斯‧維洛斯的感受？2.妳如何進行對智利的詩寫？3.自我介紹或自由談話。

　　我回答第1問：這是一個適合散步、看海和寫詩的地方。第

2問，我答：將以與聶魯達對話方式，展開一系列詩寫。臨時受訪，像突然的考試！

下午在洛斯‧維洛斯的阿爾瑪格羅學校（el liceo de almagro）大學，與師生交流。結束後，有位老師前來表示欣賞我朗讀的詩，並遞上紙條，上書簡短評論與電郵郵址，希望繼續交流，因為他也寫詩。

19:00在洛斯‧維洛斯漁民活動中心（Caleta San Pedro）朗詩。我的〈海岸〉西語版由PPdM最年輕會員Valentina Altamirano Molina（David的女兒）朗讀。我用破英文與甜美羞澀女孩交談，竟然相談甚歡，原因不外乎對詩的共同信仰。

Maggy身穿美麗舞衣，手提裙襬跳性感的哥倫比亞舞蹈cumbia。起舞後，邀李魁賢老師上台共舞，老師搖手；再向我招手，我像大部分台灣詩人一樣不會跳不敢跳。2015台南福爾摩莎國際詩歌節也有她翩翩舞影。

夜宿洛斯‧維洛斯濱海小屋。

10.24（三）第8天：喬阿帕省（Choapa）→洛斯‧維洛斯

旅途中，文字是最大的依靠；識字，是多麼幸運的事！

上午9點出發前往喬阿帕省（Choapa）至Illapel參訪文化中心，並與詩人、作家、學生座談。

再度接受媒體訪問，感謝李魁賢老師英譯，與詩人朋友Oscar的西譯！

下午到肉桂市多元高中與當地作家、詩人和當局會面。聽說這是一個清貧學校，亟待支援。詩人在擁有大面落地窗的室內圍圈，與學生詩社穿插朗讀。牆上貼有曼陀羅圖案，我因此朗讀〈曼陀羅2〉獻上祝福。貧窮使人更需詩安撫。

從洛斯·維洛斯來到此地，感覺遠離塵囂。總是用音樂提神的詩人Luis Sepulveda Castro，把我們載來羊比人多的深山（其實連羊都極少見到），山體草疏木稀，仙人掌在此找到自己的天堂；有些山密布石頭。

這裡雜貨店小小的，看起來好像甚麼食品都不缺。路邊水果攤水果好像已擺放很久，Maggy又為李老師買了檸檬、蜂蜜。我則被熟成的酪梨吸引。絲質藍天陪襯白雲棉絮，讓人總是抬頭仰望。但公園冷風使我抱胸瑟縮在椅子。

晚餐時，Maggy為感冒劇咳的李魁賢老師調了一杯蜂蜜檸檬。此行我預備的感冒藥給了李老師，可見行前備藥是必要的。

夜間行駛過山路，天空現異象——近山稜線的天邊，綿延一條雲的絲帶，幾乎貫穿整片天空，有時被山截斷。山間不知何時出現圓月，被Oscar發現，那輪明月是我所見過最大最亮的！

夜宿洛斯·維洛斯濱海小屋。

10.25（四）第9天：喬阿帕省（Choapa）學院→駱馬城（Vicuña）

上午到2013年設立的世界詩人廣場。場中一水泥台柱高約110

公分，柱頂頂面不鏽鋼板刻有PLAZA POETAS POR EL MUNDO, Los Vilos, Octubre de 2013，左上角洛斯‧維洛斯市徽，右上角世界詩人運動組織標誌。

下一站來到生態豐富的原始海岸，放眼望去，由近至遠是野草野花、海灘植被、沼澤、潮間帶、海、忽遠忽近海鳥……；另一邊由近至遠是矮坡上花花草草、廢棄鐵道、密密織成的針葉防風林，還有追逐花草忽遠忽近的我……。

11:00在喬阿帕省（Choapa）學院（College San Francisco Javier）。草坪至少躺了三條狗曬太陽，沒人敢驚動。朗讀時段，學院兩位同學開場。李魁賢老師劇咳失聲，我代讀漢語版〈金屬性的笑聲〉，西語版一貫由Oscar朗讀。

交流結束，有學生特地趕到操場向台灣詩人致謝。似乎真的有把台灣名聲傳開，竊喜！學院在校內招待午餐，從餐桌布置玫瑰鮮花到可口的食物，充分感受校方誠意。

下午往更深僻的駱馬城（Vicuña）。兩邊荒山連綿，只近處有拔地而起的綠樹，遠山近樹形成強烈而絕妙的顏色對比。不知翻過多少山頭，開車的詩人Luis Sepulveda Castro指出山間有湖，以及因此而形成的綠帶。這湖顛覆我以往對湖的刻版印象，湖隨山勢蜿蜒，時隱時現，更像一截流不出海的河段。又不知翻過多少時間，終於我們來到山高水遠的駱馬城，只為朝聖米斯特拉爾。下車後，行經一家熱鬧簡樸的理容店，獲欣然同意後拍下異國懷舊情調。

20:00，在駱馬綜合青年和成人教育中心（Centro educacional

integral de jóvenes y adultos（CEIA）Paihuen, Vicuña.Comprehensive Youth and Adult education Center），以燭光晚會方式，在學生手繪畫牆前廣場進行交流。我臨時決定台語朗讀手中華語文本〈我願意〉，結果舌頭打結！李魁賢老師因持續感冒失聲中，我代讀〈相遇是緣分〉。不知何以沒有麥克風，以致聲量難控，好吃力。

從洛斯‧維洛斯濱海小屋移棲駱馬城民宿，正慶幸房間寬敞得多，卻發現收不到網路訊息，且溫水難持久。所幸駱馬城天氣回暖。

晚餐詩人群聚民宿廚房，用Luis Arias Manzo買來的比薩果腹，一面討論此屆詩歌節，李老師替我表達回台後將以與聶魯達對話方式寫系列的詩。

10.26（五）第10天：駱馬城Leonardo da Vinci學院→米斯特拉爾故居、紀念館→埃爾桂山谷（Valle Elqui）米斯特拉爾墓園→駱馬城（Vicuña）

上午參訪駱馬城的Leonardo da Vinci學院。學校搭棚，師生坐滿校園，我懷疑是全校出動。年輕學子率先輪番上場表演不同曲風的歌，接著詩人朗詩。最後，校方頒贈一紙證書與一瓶智利紅酒給詩人。

午餐在住宿的民宿旁，guayacan餐廳有草屋頂與原住民圖騰。餐後回民宿稍事休息。下午前往不遠處米斯特拉爾故居。米斯特拉爾（Gabriela Mistral,1889-1957），1889年4月7日出生於智利埃爾桂山谷（Valla Elqui）的駱馬城（Vicuña），1957年1月10日逝於美國紐約長島。早年在駱馬山村擔任小、中學教師，後來遠至聖地亞哥智利大學、美國紐約哥倫比亞大學等學府擔任西班牙語文學教授。也是傑出外交官和教育改革者。1945年，以《柔情》獲諾貝爾文學獎，理由：「她那富於強烈感情的抒情詩歌，使她的名字成為整個拉丁美洲的理想的象徵。」她是拉丁美洲首位諾貝爾文學獎得主，也是至今唯一拉丁美洲的女性得主。1951年，獲智利國家文學獎（Premio Nacional de Literatura）。主要作品：《死亡十四行詩》、《孤寂》、《柔情》、《有刺的樹》等詩集。《死亡十四行詩》，為懷念自殺身亡的戀人而作。同性戀與未婚生子傳聞，人生暈染神祕色彩。她的學生，繼她之後榮獲諾貝爾文學獎的聶魯達推崇她是「智利的女兒，她屬於人民」。

相對於聶魯達三個陽光穿窗入房的豪宅，米斯特拉爾這深山裡的黯淡房舍何止寒酸！令我驚訝的是，人生閱歷豐富的米斯特拉爾不但不像聶魯達具無可救藥的收藏癖，從其故居看來，甚至像個身無長物的人；兩人的情感世界，一個豐富多彩，一個悲情神祕。

佇立米斯特拉爾故居，不禁揣想文學巨人少小生活景況，這般偏僻深山，駱馬城鄉親想必無法想像，他們山中貧困小女孩，來日摘下諾貝爾文學獎，好像不比摘下一顆檸檬困難。庭前樹、層層疊疊岩山、無言天空、淳樸熱情山民、背叛的情人自殺……身亡……，米斯特拉爾人生劇情似駱馬城這山路曲折。完美情人比諾貝爾文學獎更難獲致，她把情傷化成《死亡的十四行》。

　　紀念館在故居對面。相片、詩集、相關文獻……館藏豐富。具歷史情感的文物，專屬過米斯特拉爾，如今變成世人共享資產。即使文字形成隔閡，還是可以欣賞那時代書封設計的風格，從褪色的影像，還是可以捕捉那一代小孩眼裡綻放的純真光芒……。窗口，一尊米斯特拉爾半身像，面對一張小孩的大合照，突顯其教師形象。我坐雕像旁與她同面向，抬頭仰望，感受沉鬱雕像釋放無比能量。駱馬城春風撫過窗口，她的臉，我的臉。我把米斯特拉爾裝進心裡，帶回我的台北；雕像留給駱馬城。

　　從故居所在駱馬城，翻山越嶺方抵達其任教學校——埃爾桂山谷（Valle Elqui）的蒙特葛蘭德（Montegrande）。昔日交通不便，人是如何移動，尤其在此偏鄉中的偏鄉？其任教學校設置的米斯特拉爾紀念室占地不廣、文物不多，但擁有最榮耀的諾貝爾獎牌。

　　從學校走一段路、爬一段陡坡，才抵達米斯特拉爾墓園，園中有其雕像。詩人在此朗詩，可惜我尚未寫詩致敬。

　　19:00乘車盤旋而上，到達寸草不生，只剩一棵樹的一大片空地。天色漸暗，星星開始浮現。往人群聚集處緩步移動，原來是在天文導覽。台灣詩人完全聽不懂。站到腳痠，詩人團開始往車停處移動，雖星星滿天，地面卻異常黑暗，Maggy打開手機照明，我攙扶重感冒的老師如履薄冰走過崎嶇不平又有亂石的坡面。好不容易蹭到車旁，站在越來越冷的風中，在難以站立的坡面，最後我脫下高跟鞋倚著車身。不知道為什麼月亮還不出現。不遠處有人升起營火。晚餐是一個漢堡夾沒調味的乾肉。上山發生的這一切應是屬於高中或大學生的浪漫。枯等到11點，我認定月亮不會出現，鑽入車中避寒休息。後來大家都上車，我鬆了一口氣，以為終於要回民宿，因為翌日移棲，夜間又得熬夜打包。不料車行不遠即煞住，但神奇的是月亮竟從山的裂縫慢慢慢慢出現，又亮又圓的滿月！生平第一次等待月出，而且花這麼長時間，此時所有的不耐煩盡釋。其他詩人伸長脖子競相對月狼嚎。

10.27（六）第11天：駱馬城→塞廉納（La Serena）→科金博（Coquimbo）海岸→聖地亞哥Carlton旅館

詩歌節最後一天。在智利這些日子，我幾乎不吃早餐，今天Maggy為我留了一顆蘋果，教我感動。民宿不供早餐，這兩天Maggy與助理Tatiana Milena Gomez為詩人備早點。

09:00，兩部車載著國際詩人奔回出發地聖地亞哥。大約10點抵達科金博首府塞廉納（La Serena）。海岸一白色巨塔矗立在小型城堡中。隔一大片沙地才能抵達海邊，有小女孩在沙浴。遲疑半天，我還是蹬著高跟鞋走過這一大片沙地。慶幸自己有走到水邊，海水滋潤的沙灘散置貝殼，這些貝殼雖不上相，但都能享受到激情浪濤聲，與浪花熱情擁抱。聽說這裡曾發生海嘯。

中午到達科金博（Coquimbo）海岸，坡道邊岩石峭壁矗立，荒涼中點綴龍舌蘭、仙人掌、雜草、野花……，充滿粗獷之美，再往前更有無遮蔽的海景，山海之間風景一剛一柔。風格迥異於黑島，兩者我都收藏進回憶的倉庫。最後詩人全爬上古砲台陣地的守望台上，詩歌節的詩人海報已張貼在壁上，變成美景的一部分。陽光刺眼、海風陣陣，Luis Arias Manzo一一唱名頒發詩歌節出席證。

David Altamirano Hernandez以記者身分訪問我對智利印象。我答：「智利是一個美麗的國家，雖然台灣也很美，但智利風景更多樣。」如此回答並不周延，我應該說智利多了台灣所沒有的沙漠（此行未進入阿他加馬沙漠），其他山光水色各有千秋。接著被問會不會再度來訪，我回答：「當然會，智利人開朗、樂觀、幽默，我覺得與智利人相處非常愉快」，這確是心裡話。

午餐在魚市場吃簡餐。

回到聖地亞哥，重返原先入住的旅館Carlton，但因未預約，房間不夠，以致Oscar René Benítez、Jose Rolando Bedoya Avalos跟著Luis Arias Manzo與Maggy夫婦住到其他旅館。發生這樣的事，台灣人百思不解。

自始至終負責開車，十分貼心的紳士詩人Luis Sepulveda Castro跟我道別，我以為會再見於餞別宴，後來才知他轉頭就開車回返家鄉洛斯·維洛斯。我曾有幾天坐他旁邊，他總是用西班牙語夾英語為我介紹沿途景物，遇到馬、羊也暫停指給我看。更有一次，見路邊有人坐地不起，他特地下車幫忙攙扶。

詩人們從旅館步行到鬧區餐館吃簡餐惜別宴。

住到有客廳廚房的大房間，可惜一滴熱水都出不來，只好洗冷水，偏偏聖地亞哥氣溫偏低。這樣的事也會特別難忘！

10.28（日）第12天：聖地亞哥市區→機場

最後一天台灣詩人與入住同旅館的詩人Susana Goldemberg、Arcelia Cruces de Axipuru、Lorena Aixpuru參加聖地亞哥市內觀光。搭纜車的行程，引發年邁的阿根廷女詩人拍手歡呼。憑票上遊覽車，遊客可選任一停靠站下車觀光，再到沿途站點上車。車經新市區，摩登高樓大廈令我讚歎。其實我對現代摩天大樓從無好感，但這城市的新建物像在比賽造型創意，每一棟都獨具特色，使我不得不佩服背後的建築師。

原本下午Luis Arias Manzo要送李老師、我，以及Oscar到機場，後來因為分居不同旅館，李老師與我得自己叫計程車，最後我們與墨西哥母女Arcelia Cruces de Axipuru、Lorena Aixpuru共乘一部計程車。還沒要返國的Susana Goldemberg特地到小小的大廳與我們吻別。

在機場下車後與墨西哥母女詩人道別，看到Arcelia Cruces de Axipuru就要流淚，我忍住在眼眶打轉的淚水。進機場不久，Luis Arias Manzo意外出現，他上前來說Maggy與Oscar也在機場，陪我們處理好登機之事，隨即離去尋找墨西哥母女。好不容易把這些人加上哥倫比亞詩人Jose Rolando Bedoya Avalos都兜在一起了，Maggy抱著我流淚許久。流淚，使心融合！

山海之間

在智利一邊靠山一邊瀕海的路程，總被異國新奇景觀觸動。

感動，始於機上看日出。日出前，天空披戴紅橙黃色帶，黑色山脈像木炭被一撮紅光熨燙，火紅一點一點擴散；稜線不只有金色，還伴有紅、綠兩條金絲線，第一次看到這奇景，懷疑自己眼睛，是否看到海市蜃樓；腳下連綿沙漠清晰可見……，美景瑰麗如夢，難以描摹。

絲帶狀智利國土，擁有綿長海岸線，沙灘、岩礁不缺，海浪澎湃，甚至曾發生海嘯。如此激情的海，難怪產生熱情的人與詩！

智利山脈迥異於四季常綠的台灣山巒。從聖地亞哥北行，山體沒有覆蓋濃密高壯的樹林，山腳下才有帶狀喬木。遠觀，山坡好像散布黑羊；近看，是稀疏的矮木短草。

從洛斯‧維洛斯往駱馬城的深山，遠觀光禿，近看可見稀疏仙人掌。一路上常呈荒山與高聳翠綠近樹強烈對比。光禿山脈（近看也許有疏短植被）並不單調乏味，完全不會造成視覺疲乏，因在光影中，山的肌理線條呈現異樣的美，尤其入暮之前，遠山轉成光滑淡紫，層層山巒各具本色，壯麗非凡！

我不解的是，到處荒山野地，智利的農業在哪裡？

智利地廣人稀，平房組成社區，街巷遍植綠樹，視野遼闊；唯一亂源是電線。

智利男人習慣站在車門口扶女性一把，即使是頭髮已翻白的

161

老紳士。初時我不習慣，因為台灣並不如此，等到習慣，又要折返舊巢。他們也容易一見鍾情，而且當街送飛吻，當眾朗讀現寫情詩示愛。

智利小孩從小就習慣被擁抱被親吻，溫暖的肢體語言，的確讓人互相貼近，獲得慰藉。所到之處，不論老少都會自動跟我打招呼。智利人對老弱婦孺十分呵護，充分彰顯人性之美。智利學子充滿自信，有禮而不拘謹，我感受到校園氣氛十分自由浪漫，我很羨慕這種處處有愛的文化。

回首詩歌節

頂著被三度提名諾貝爾文學獎光環，以及一本《給智利的情詩20首》，李魁賢老師所到之處備受禮遇，每場交流幾乎都是打頭陣，接著是坐在旁邊的我；他成為主角，被特別介紹，甚至被推崇為「台灣的聶魯達」。我也每場都被介紹為「台灣詩人」，台灣名號因此銘刻智利人、國際詩人的心。

第一次踏上智利，我最大障礙仍是語言，幸好帶了漢英西三語詩集《保證》到各地交流，西語朗讀則有賴南美人幫忙。李老師有遠見，一直從事詩的翻譯，也幫國內詩人出版外語詩集。

行前詩人林鷺告訴我說：「詩人去智利意義非凡」、「這是身為詩人最好的禮物」、「聶魯達的故鄉確實是身為詩人該瞻仰的聖地」，我很幸運被贈予這份幸福的禮物。

2014年，李魁賢老師首次帶詩人團踏上智利參加詩歌節，寫了一本《給智利的情詩20首》，此次帶到智利朗讀給智利人聽，別具意義。詩的朝聖之旅，第8天我寫下：「旅途中，文字是最大的依靠；識字，是多麼幸運的事！」因為文字媒介，我才得以寫詩、讀詩，朝向詩人之路；我已向智利承諾，將以與聶魯達對話方式，寫一系列的詩。上帝會不會再次送我一份厚禮——帶著《親愛的聶魯達》到聶魯達故居朗讀？

作者簡介

　　陳秀珍，淡江大學中國文學系畢業。1998年開始以筆名林弦在《中外文學》、《文學台灣》、《淡水牛津文藝》和《台灣新文學》等刊物發表詩作，現為《笠》詩社同仁。出版散文集《非日記》（2009年）、詩集《林中弦音》（2010年）、《面具》（2016年）、《不確定的風景》（2017年）、《保證》（2017年，漢英西三語）、《淡水詩情》、《骨折》（2018年，台華雙語）等。

　　詩入選英西漢三語《兩半球詩路》（Poetry Road Between Two Hemispheres, 2015）、西班牙語《以詩為證》（Opus Testimoni, 2017）、義大利語《對話》（Dialoghi, 2017）與《翻譯筆記本》（Quaderni di traduzione, 2018）、西英漢三語《台灣心聲》（2017）、漢英土三語版《台灣心聲》（2018）、《soflay的耳語》（2018年度詩歌詩集第2卷）、Amaravati版《詩的三稜鏡》2018詩選集等、《21世紀兩岸詩歌鑑藏（戊戌卷）》（2019）。詩

另被譯成孟加拉文、阿爾巴尼亞文、馬其頓文、土耳其文、越南文、羅馬尼亞文、印地文、尼泊爾文、信德文、希伯來文等。

參加2015年台南福爾摩莎國際詩歌節，2016年孟加拉卡塔克（Kathak）詩高峰會、第20屆馬其頓奈姆日（Ditët e Naimit）國際詩歌節、2016~2019年淡水福爾摩莎國際詩歌節，2017年祕魯第18屆【柳葉黑野櫻、巴列霍及其土地】（Capulí Vallejo y su Tierra）國際詩歌節，2018年突尼西亞第5屆西迪‧布塞（Sidi Bou Saïd）國際詩歌節、2018年第14屆智利【詩人軌跡】（Tras las Huellas del Poeta）國際詩歌節、2019年第3屆越南國際詩歌節、2019年羅馬尼亞第6屆雅西市（Iasi）國際詩歌節。2019年墨西哥第1屆鳳凰巢國際詩歌節。獲得2018年【柳葉黑野櫻、巴列霍及其土地】（Capulí Vallejo y su Tierra）清晨之星獎。2020年黎巴嫩納吉‧納曼文學獎（Lebanon Naji Naaman Literary Prizes 2020.）。

譯者簡介

　　李魁賢，1937年生，1953年開始發表詩作，曾任台灣筆會會長，國家文化藝術基金會董事長。現任國際作家藝術家協會理事、世界詩人運動組織副會長、福爾摩莎國際詩歌節策劃。詩被譯成各種語文在日本、韓國、加拿大、紐西蘭、荷蘭、南斯拉夫、羅馬尼亞、印度、希臘、美國、西班牙、巴西、蒙古、俄羅斯、立陶宛、古巴、智利、尼加拉瓜、孟加拉、馬其頓、土耳其、波蘭、塞爾維亞、葡萄牙、馬來西亞、義大利、墨西哥、摩洛哥等國發表。

　　出版著作包括《李魁賢詩集》全6冊、《李魁賢文集》全10冊、《李魁賢譯詩集》全8冊、翻譯《歐洲經典詩選》全25冊、《名流詩叢》38冊、李魁賢回憶錄《人生拼圖》和《我的新世紀詩路》，及其他共二百餘本。英譯詩集有《愛是我的信仰》、《溫柔的美感》、《島與島之間》、《黃昏時刻》、《存在或不存在》和《感應》。詩集《黃昏時刻》被譯成英文、蒙古文、俄羅斯文、羅馬尼亞文、西班牙文、法文、韓文、孟加拉文、塞爾維亞文、阿爾巴尼亞文、土耳其文，以及有待出版的馬其頓文、德文、阿拉伯文等。

曾獲韓國亞洲詩人貢獻獎、榮後台灣詩獎、賴和文學獎、行政院文化獎、印度麥氏學會詩人獎、吳三連獎新詩獎、台灣新文學貢獻獎、蒙古文化基金會文化名人獎牌和詩人獎章、蒙古建國八百週年成吉思汗金牌、成吉思汗大學金質獎章和蒙古作家聯盟推廣蒙古文學貢獻獎、真理大學台灣文學家牛津獎、韓國高麗文學獎、孟加拉卡塔克文學獎、馬其頓奈姆‧弗拉謝里文學獎、祕魯特里爾塞金獎和金幟獎、台灣國家文藝獎、印度普立哲書商首席傑出詩獎。

My Beloved
Neruda

CONTENTS

A pilgrimage of love

——Foreword to Chen Hsiu-Chen's My Beloved Neruda

By Lin Lu

Since time immemorial, love has been a old yet also fresh topic. The definition of love is sometimes noble, other times humble; the trials of love is sometimes magnificent, other times cruel. Love really makes people look upwards, but also often make people pause and sigh in their step. Some have wondered if poetry of love becomes overly abundant, whether they will be like fading roses, without color or fragrance. One can get an amazing answer to this question if one looks at the poetess Chen Hsiu-Chen, who uses love as the goalpost, and continue to create new works. It is often said that people often love to praise the love poems of the Nobel Laureate winner, where countless poets has attempted to climb the peak of love poems that grew out of Neruda's natural disposition. When a poetess that champions love finally step onto the land where Neruda was born and grew up in 2018, and visited Neruda's three former abodes, one should be more than curious what kind of love poems she has composed in her 66-poem collection "My Beloved Neruda".

In his work, A Midsummer's Night Dream, Shakespeare wrote:

"Lovers and madmen have such seething brains,

Such shaping fantasies, that apprehend.

More than cool reason ever comprehends.

The lunatic, the lover and the poet."

Indeed, the phrases of love are often generated by the imagination. The deep and explicit conveyance of emotions by poets is extracted from the rich imagination of poetry. This is how I view Chen Hsiu-Chen's journey to Chile, and see it rather as her pilgrimage of love. The journey starts from the restless murmur of "Oh, my Neruda/ I am afraid/ I would love you so/ as the waves love the rocks along the coast/ to crush myself." and flies to arrive at "The Sky of Neruda" that poets long for.

The poet land from the sky carry the love in the heart, just as the warmth in the time and space of "The sunset imitates a red light", and curtain raises on the first scene through the lines of "Duo": "Oh, my Neruda,/ at the wonderful time and space in Chile/ you used your native language/ I use my native language/ to recite a love poem in duo."

And lets love in the passion of "At night/ my body sprouts abruptly.", to become committed to the conflict of "Cold Sea Breeze" where Neruda's former residence on Isla Negra faces the ocean, and become the humble lover that yells out:"Oh, my Neruda,/ I am calling you for the necessary nutrients./

The sprouted new bud is going to sacrifice itself/ to grow into a fragrant rose/ leaving red to Isla Negra/ and fragrance to the springtime."

The worship of love always begins from the embrace of love, such as this poem below:

"In Your Embrace"

In your embrace
I become a boat
giving up the wind and sail,
mooring in your gentle harbor.

In your embrace
I become a tame white pigeon
giving up the whole sky,
to have you as my wings.

In your embrace
I lose my direction,
and depend on two torches of your eyes
to navigate me in the endless night.

In your embrace

my whole body is transformed into one ear

without hearing the beasts roaring to me,

but only listening to your whisper.

In your embrace

I automatically disarm my gun and bullets.

You have so powerful weapon

that I am willing to be hurt by you.

Oh, my Neruda,

I will spend my exclusive life

to exchange with you

an embrace in everlasting love.

The poet's full and intense emotions can even be seen in "no cumbersome visa is necessary to my dreamland/ rather a free evaluation of the evidence./ I promise you free entry/ for hundred/ or thousand times.", lines from the poem "At Dusk", promising infinite tolerance that she gives to love.

The imageries in Chen Hsiu-Chen's poems have often been complex and versatile, with deep meanings and intense emotions in the poems, but the language is not overly difficult. Basically, I believe when one read her poems, it is easy to be drawn in by the feelings overflowing in her poetry. Let me list a few examples as evidence:

"I, as a wooden woman,/ have been drunk,/ becoming a string of plump grapes/ to be brewed/ into a bottle of red wine/ with high alcohol content" — "Red Wine"

"When the earrings are lost/ the earlobes return to freedom./ Why your ears still from time to time/ resound jingle bells from/ the earrings? " — "Earrings"

"I imagined the stars/ being your smiling eyes/ the crystal shards splashing out of there in a blink/ were adhered on the black satin canopy./ Since then/ I have loved night more than daytime." — "Stars"

"In deep night of early spring/ I pulled on winter coats one by one/ like an onion/ buried into a thick quilt as black soil/ waiting for sunrise / let me sprout." — "Cold"

"ambiguous love/ is happy,/ please don't use your whisper/ your spell/ to deliver my love." — "Love"

If love only brings a simple sort of happiness, then the feelings are probably not profound, and it may even be impossible for love poems worthy of praise to be created. The love poems written by Chen Hsiu-Chen has all the quintessential element of love, such as "Oh, my Neruda,/ the dream fangs finished chewing the starry sky all night/ then turned around to chew/ the Adam's ribs deserted to me/ that makes me a drastic pain/ indescribable." in "The Dream", "Oh, my Neruda,/ I didn't become that lake unable flowing to the sea/ or that tree doing nothing but absent minded./ I have experienced many lonely sunsets/ and finally arriving at the land of poets./ If you are a stone mountain/ I will turn into a seed/ to be planted into your body/ becoming your bone." in "Moving Forward to Vicuña", and "At midnight/ I'm blown into your dream to take an adventure./ Your bow and arrows are laid aside apparently,/ why I was injured all over my body." as well as "Oh, my Neruda,/ you are the hunter getting something for nothing/ and I must be healed deep in your / soul." in "Pale Purple", all using beautiful, poetic imageries to deliver the anxiety, pain and sorrow that love carves into one's heart to the souls of the readers.

I should remind the readers that they should not limit Chen Hsiu-Chen's love poems to only the imagination of love between the sexes, because the feelers her poems extends out has special, macro perspectives. She has the ability to utilize the various scenarios and setting she absorbed, to use different language styles and transform them into rich, emotive poetic phrasing. From this collection, I was also able to read about her footsteps that were stretched forth by love. For example, when she visited the former residence of Chile's first Nobel Laureate, Gabriel Mistral, she wrote "Love is / harder to win than Nobel prize in literature./ How many tears have been wept / in writing your Sonnets of Death,/ I secretly wiped off your grief / that your tears have wetted/ my heart."seen in"Gabriela Mistral's Old House"; after visiting the grave of the Chilean poet, Vicente Huidobro, who is also an advocate of the Creacionismo movement, she used the last line from Huidobro's poem Arte Poética -"the poet is a little god" and turned it into the "Dreamland" of "Oh, poet/ you are a little god./ I wish/ to live in your genesis."; or the poem dedicated to the Chilean poet Oscar Castro "Among the lily's fragrance under moonlight/ your loneliness/ exactly has kissed/ my loneliness./ I devoted the rose/ to accompany you/ in your sound sleep." in "I devoted the Rose". These are all love poems for describe her love for these poets based on the fundamentals of love.

I also noticed that Chen Hsiu-Chen has also wrote a fair number of love poems based on the love of the country, and on the numerous overseas visit in the name of poetry, she has not forgotten her homeland. In "Admiration of Light, No. 2" appeared these lines:

Oh, my Neruda,

you lived in a stable life,

Spain is in your heart*.

You countered against a great dark age

by means of a bit of fluorescence.

In your fluorescence

I think

how to become a firefly.

Taiwan is in my heart

Chen Hsiu-Chen is like an energized, active volcano of love that continues to erupt with new works. She has wrote many poems that are worthy of reading for those who are in love, or who have forgotten love; but not only that, should Neruda, the king of love poems, who the kingdom of love worships, discover there is a talent poetess in the distant East who uses phrases that similar tugs on the heart and sings in response about the love that he lauds, he would surely be moved to tears. I do not recall which poet said this, "Life is a scenery, and love is a bouquet of flowers. Without flowers, the scenery will not be glorious. Without love, life can easily become a barren land." I would like to use a few lines line from the poem "The Country at Horizon"

At my middle age

you have lit up my life map with poetry.

Where will I be for the time being

if I have not met you,

which planet will I pilgrim toward

if have not encountered with you?

to wish all the people in this world can successfully find their own star of love that they would worship on their life's journeys!

(English Translation by Te-chang Mike Lo)

The Sky of Neruda

The wind

tears off the notices from autumn one by one

that posted in the form of red maple leaves.

My heart in despair listens to

your one hundred love poems

The spring is in the distance.

I heard someone calling

a sound after a sound.

An ocean is hidden secretly in my heart.

From the Taiwan island

I am flying to the sky of Neruda

to praise in a high key

the love sonnets.

Oh, my Neruda,

I love you

as a Forgetting-me-not loves the May.

Oh, my Neruda

I am afraid

I would love you so

as the waves love the rocks along the coast

to crush myself.

Chile in October

In October
I accepted an accidental grace
with full hand of fallen leaves in the autumn wind
and close my eyes in thinking about the opposite bank of
Pacific Ocean becoming a romantic spring season.

Isla Negra*¹ sounded with your excited waves
Santiago*² remained many of your loving memories
Valparaiso*³ having left your secluded house
could be my temporary refuge?

Oh, my Neruda,
my footsteps will become
the momentary collection in your residence.

What kind of flowery love letters will be issued at first
among numerous woken trees and grasses

in the Spring time of Chile

to strand my

dazzling eyes

and to excite my heart.

*[1] Neruda lived in Isla Negra time after time.
*[2] La Chascona, the former residence of Neruda situates at Santiago.
*[3] La Sebastiana, another residence of Neruda situates at Valparasio.

Duo

The sunset imitates a red light

hung on the sky.

At night

The sea surface is looked like a solidified sky shade

while the sky photocopies the white tides.

Oh, my Neruda,

at the wonderful time and space in Chile

you used your native language

I use my native language

to recite a love poem in duo.

At this moment

just like sea and sky translate to each other

the sound of tide resonates

in deep valley between two hearts.

White Deer

Three years ago
at Sun Moon Lake
I heard with enlarging ears
the recital by exotic poets.
Among the floral fragrance
my trembled hands capture
a poetic white deer
hidden within luxuriant leaves.

At present
I read my poem softly
and surprise
to capture
the white deer lost once.

Oh, my Neruda,
I am afraid

the white deer that regained

would be again trapped into a cloudy wrong path,

I am afraid

my white deer will indulge in the clouds.

The clouds are raised from

two lakes of my eyes.

White deer, oh, white deer

don't give up me once more

without regard.

In Your Embrace

In your embrace
I become a boat
giving up the wind and sail,
mooring in your gentle harbor.

In your embrace
I become a tame white pigeon
giving up the whole sky,
to have you as my wings.

In your embrace
I lose my direction,
and depend on two torches of your eyes
to navigate me in the endless night.

In your embrace
my whole body is transformed into one ear

without hearing the beasts roaring to me,

but only listening to your whisper.

In your embrace

I automatically disarm my gun and bullets.

You have so powerful weapon

that I am willing to be hurt by you.

Oh, my Neruda,

I will spend my exclusive life

to exchange with you

an embrace in everlasting love.

Cold Sea Breeze

Cold sea breeze
penetrates into my skin pores
pouring into the respiratory tract
to freeze me becoming
a tree thoroughly awaken.

At night
my body sprouts abruptly.

Oh, my Neruda,
I am calling you for the necessary nutrients.
The sprouted new bud is going to sacrifice itself
to grow into a fragrant rose
leaving red to Isla Negra
and fragrance to the springtime.

Whisper

The white flowers
fly like snow.
The clop-clop sounds of high heels
stepped on a row of flowering trees
have dipped a luxurious floral smell.

It sounds like a Illusion
or a spell
Forget me not! Forget me not! Forget me not!
Is it the whisper from the petals
or the voices suppressed in my deep heart?

Oh, my Neruda,
under the starry sky of Santiago
my heart blooms like snow,
its petals are going to drift into your heart.

Forget Me

Not only the white flowers

even that red, orange, yellow and purple wildflowers

also under encouragement by the spring breeze

compete to one another in murmuring

in murmuring to me:

Forget me not! Forget me not! Forget me not!

Not only the waves or seabirds

even the leaves also under the silver moonlight

whisper to me

Forget me not! Forget me not! Forget me not!

Not only the valleys or hills

even the stars, moon and sun

also whisper to me uninterruptedly

Forget me not! Forget me not! Forget me not!

Oh, my Neruda,

It is you the only one in the world

have not confessed to me yet:

Forget me not! Oh,

Forget me not!

The Eyes in Santiago

———at La Chascona

The eyes are everywhere
as the narks arranged
here and there.

Like overbearing eyes of
a strict lover
in the inner room or garden
to test whether love is
persistent or not.

The eyes seem
being restrained by desire
to look for
a blind love.

Oh, my Neruda,
there are so many eyes,

eye, eye, eye.

Which one is mine?

Which one is yours?

Can we combine to form a pair of eyes

staring at the same star?

I deliberate to capture you

but afraid, instead,

to be captured by you.

* In La Chascona, the former residence of Neruda, there are many
   totems of eyes indoors and outdoors.

Earrings

When the earrings are lost
the earlobes return to freedom.
Why your ears still from time to time
resound jingle bells from
the earrings?

The earrings, when detained by
the ear holes, make a witness
that it has no wisdom to judge
what will be happened about the real heart of lover
before drying up of the sea and decay of the stone
as so many promises under a vow.

When missed
or called by someone
the ears will be itchy
just like an acute inflammation.

Whether the earrings

will be used to regaining freedom

or will miss the vow in the ears

day and night?

Oh, my Neruda,

the vow is a spring breeze

that the earrings have been waiting

for vibration by it at any time.

At Dusk

The trees
lift their thousand hands and fingers high
to capture the tired birds.

From the sparse forest
there are light-emitting eyes
in peeking.
We are sitting in the car to count
the eyes
the eyes more and more.

During the journey of slight vibration
like in a cradle slowly shaken
the night atmosphere becomes a valid amulet.
I am seeking
a broad shoulder for my head to rest
as a warm bed in my dream.

Oh, my Neruda,

no cumbersome visa is necessary to my dreamland

rather a free evaluation of the evidence.

I promise you free entry

for hundred

or thousand times.

Graffiti

Along the steep slope in Valparaiso
a graffiti street
is painted with colorful drawings
without any blank vacancy,
showing optimistic characters
of Latin American.

The graffiti
on the walls one after another
tell respective colorful story in competition.
Even the old houses
still have a youthful face
displaying no age spots.

Oh, my Neruda,
my fracture caused by car accident
left a dark purple scar on my leg

deeply depressed

looked like an ugly lane.

I should learn to imitate Chilean people

to draw on my scars

a graffito with one red rose.

Shading

——Seabirds at Isla Negra

On the Pacific shore
I clearly heard
a seabird
flapping its wings definitely
to declare a fiery love toward the sky.

At Isla Negra
this seabird has once abandoned whole sky
now flushes with two wings to shade
its shy face
and cringing feet.

Oh, my Neruda,
in your boundless blue sky
you cannot see
even impossible to imagine
its skillful flying.

Moonrise at Vicuña

Our car climbed to higher altitude
arriving at the high mountain
earlier than the first star.

Millions of stars are all present
still waiting for no full moon.
Some stars are sleeping
some stars have caught cold
some stars turned to blue.

Raise a campfire burnt to become the sun.
Drink red wine to warm the love in avoidance of drowsiness.
Oh, my Neruda,
has the moon already abandoned whole sky?

I am about to close my eyes
giving up to wait

wait for the abandoned moon

suddenly projecting out of the depression of distant mountains

a pure gold brilliant ray.

Ah

more and more stars are all crying.

Full moon illuminates

my ear that was cut by the crescent moon during my childhood.

Moonlight induces the poets to display inherent essence

in stretching their necks and opening their big bloody mouths.

The poets sound the wolf howls

shaking the valley at Vicuña.

Golden moon not swallowed by wolves

still guards

the dream in springtime at Vicuña.

Isla Negra

The sky embraces the ocean,
the ocean kisses the heaven.

Exciting vocal cords of the tides
are unable to cover up
the streaming footsteps of your beloved and yourself.
Push aside the romantic weaving white quilt,
leave the pillow for diving morning sun,
your heartbeat is clearly heard.

How can you firm your believe
in the secret hidden within love?
The secret is a mysterious gift packaged
in a cloud paper placed under the Christmas tree
inducing each hand
a desire to peek.

I break into your original private residence.

Oh, my Neruda,

please tell me about

the secret hidden within your love.

I have opened my ears

as large as the sky.

I heard

the rolling waves

constantly hitting the rocks with naked figure.

Memorial Museum

I gazed

every face caught on camera,

the face in meeting

the face at farewell.

I heard

the streaming footsteps,

there are wild flowers occupying the cape in spring

at Isla Negra,

the combination of colorful houses along hillside

at Valparaiso,

and residence decorated with many eyes

at Santiago.

The fishes

try to hold the steps of the waves,

the waves instead
keep running towards the shore.

Oh, my Neruda,
the little space in my heart room
has turned into a complex memorial museum.
I hope the lost fawn
not turning back
to disturb my heart.

Collections

In the house full of collections

you and lover sat side by side

at intimate chairs along a table

sharing warm coffee

under either the sweet morning light

or lazy moment at dusk,

maybe also share a little bit sadness.

Love affair is sometime tinged with gray and blue.

At the residence without you

your unclear footsteps

approach to me step by step

for guiding me to your favorite collections

that you collected for many years.

I listen the double strings of love

in resonance just like two hearts throbbing.

I watch the love in tango

appearing the shadows of roses and yourself.

Oh, my Neruda,

among your tremendous collections

what makes me most jealousy

is your firm believe in love.

Your love

is never ceased.

I manage to steal

one lovely line

from your love poems

to dissolve it

into golden liquor today.

Red Wine

The ocean brewed by time

becomes a pool of charming wine

making my eyes

drunk

at dusk.

A refill of wine

makes my intestines, my stomach

and my stony heart

drunk.

I, as a wooden woman,

have been drunk,

becoming a string of plump grapes

to be brewed

into a bottle of red wine

with high alcohol content.

Oh, my Neruda,

drink me up

let me occupy you

like a fish possesses an entire ocean.

Laughing

The stars are overcrowded on the sky
while the waves are dancing over the sea.

Pass the laughter to the stars
let the song dance with white waves
let the sound of love
full fill every black hole in life.

Please sing Happy Birthday loudly
sing Happy New Year at high key.
Happy Birthday!
Happy New Year!
Because after departure
the silence is as long as the coastline
the blank is as big as sky of Isla Negra.

Sing
with my dialect
and your dialect
Happy Birthday!
Happy New Year!

Oh, my Neruda,
we laugh in our sweet happy
with salty tears.

Sunrise

Before sunrise
the red brilliant light
burns a mountain,
like burning a big black charcoal
getting the fire more and more stronger.
After cooling
it remains
a deep burning pain.

Oh, my Neruda,
the vision of sunrise stays temporarily
but why
stays so long
that the whole sky and earth
have cooled down as the black charcoal,
and my eyes
even my mind
are still seized by a red sun.

Secrets in Love

You believe
the secret hidden in love,
Oh, my Neruda,
the biggest secret hidden in love
is a secret lover.

To your beloved
you highlight her with numerous secret psalms
while cover her with a black curtain.

Anonymous "Los Versos del capitán"
cannot be kept secret by any camouflage.
You finally open the buds
to release rose petals.
Love becomes the sweet desert in your life
and secrets become the sweet desert of your love.

Suppose

the secret lasts forever,

will the ending be a tragedy?

On the Tip of the Tongue

The red wine
on the tip of the tongue
blushes many
flushed facial masks.

My verse
on the tip of the tongue
grows up
pleasant and smooth.

Oh, my Neruda,
my love
does not perform duet dance
on the tip of the tongue.

My love
is hidden deep inside

lonely

to sing alone

a lonely song.

You will never hear the lyric

of the loneliness

unless

you direct your ears

deep into my heart.

My Rose

—Reciting my poem "The Story of Rose" in Chile

I brought rose in privacy

flying to South America.

Chilean people saw my rose

and read my rose poem.

My rose

breathed the golden sunshine at Viña del Mar

and dispersed fragrance

spreading murmur of a lot of retroflex.

Since then, there is a rose story to be continued.

I wore rose petals

shy of entering into your Isla Negra.

Oh, my Neruda,

I want to plant my rose

in your eye socket,

your earhole,

your nasal cavity,

your pen core and your deep dream.

I planted my rose

in your present day, your tomorrow,

all your life.

Before you tattoo with rose

the rose will wash your soul

with a thousand drops of tear.

The Country at Horizon

I flied across the thousands miles on clouds
arriving at the country at horizon.

A pair of lightning eyes
chased a timid little goat
on top of the cliff.
The passionate conversations among waves
are broadcasting along the Pacific Coast

Has been there an arrangement unconsciously?
The country of poets,
the continuous stone mountains and unlimited sea
inspire me again and again
more imagination.

At my middle age
you have lit up my life map with poetry.

Where will I be for the time being

if I have not met you,

which planet will I pilgrim toward

if have not encountered with you?

Oh, my Neruda,

I am glad

inclining to the arrangement settled unconsciously.

The letter is my original and final residence

where the endless of happiness born.

Light Envelopes Me

Oh, my Neruda,

I used to paint

my face a heavy makeup by falsehood .

Under your gaze

my glorious makeup keeps peeling off

as faded flower, on the ground.

Light envelops me

from top to toe

makes me, in bloom

from outside to inside.

Ah, the spring is coming.

Time is Born of the Clock

Time is born of the clock.

During labor pain

long and short hands of the clock meet, one moment,

long and short hands of the clock separate, the other.

I keep silent within time

while something in past time is chattering.

I wait in silence

for flowers going to bloom,

long and short hands of time

like a sharp scissors

cutting off sorrow and also laughter.

Oh, my Neruda,

under the sky of your poetry

one of my eyes

to see separation

another to watch reunion.

Rose and Cactus

Red rose
and white cactus
love you at the same time.
Oh, my Neruda,
the only fertile soil in your heart
will decide whom to dedicate.

The rose,
a considerate flower,
disperses its female fragrance.
The cactus,
shy, pure and refined,
hides its flowery love words within deep heart.

When you hold the cactus
do you miss rose and its sweet smile?

When you embrace the rose
may you secretly regret for the cactus?

The rose has thorns
the cactus has spines too.
Does your fingers hesitate
there between to select
and eventually
plant both exotic flowers
into your unbounded verse.

Cactus

Far away from flowers and herbs

the cactus

searches for its own paradise

at badlands in the remote stone mountain.

For fear of hurting

the cactus learns from hedgehog

dressing up military uniform

on the alert in full attention

to bloom pure and humble white flowers

under the calling of the sun.

Same as the rose,

the cactus says,

love

is what my paradise.

Oh, my Neruda,

are you ready to pick this

thorny love flower?

Cactus is Praying

The cactus

is praying to the sky without a cloud

but still

no rain falls.

Whether crying is

easier than praying

to be heard by God?

But the cactus has not learned

how to cry since ancient times up to date.

The cactus just persists

to pray in the morning

also in the evening.

I have overheard it.

Oh, my Neruda,

I prayed for your coming in the season without you.

親愛的聶魯達
My Beloved Neruda

I learned to use your language

to pray on sunny day

also on rainy day.

You are more difficult than God to hear

my mumbling prayer on my knees.

I learned from the cactus

keep going on praying.

The prayer may be a gust of wind

waking your ears at once

at a certain instant.

The Cacti on Barren Mountains

The cacti
when forced to marginal area
still keep peaceful in nature
fond of standing dry on remote barren mountains.

The cacti with spines
dissimilar to common flowering trees
have not hundreds of gentle fingers
to touch or to be touched by the spring breeze.

Forgotten by bees and butterflies
also forgotten by clouds and rains
do the cacti have spring season themselves?

Bright seasons
and dark seasons
come and go for bringing nothing

sadness or joy to the barren mountains.

The autistic stones are

rosary of the cacti one after another.

Oh, my Neruda,

when the cacti are blooming

you will surprise to find out

that the cacti are not stone sculptures.

Stars

In night driving, we passed by
Vicuña*¹ in silent stone mountain area,
and Los Vilos*² seashore with high tides.
My action of lifting eyes and stepping forward
have been watched by the stars,
my monologues
have been all heard by the stars.
Even my almost tripping up to pick a rose
has been also remembered by the stars.

I imagined the stars
being your smiling eyes
the crystal shards splashing out of there in a blink
were adhered on the black satin canopy.
Since then
I have loved night more than daytime.

親愛的聶魯達

My Beloved Neruda

Oh, my Neruda,

in such sweet boundless

unlimited illusory blue night,

my beautiful dream under the warm quilt

cannot be seen

even the stars shine more brilliant.

*[1] Vicuña, a small town in northern Chile.
*[2] Los Vilos, a small town in northern Chile.

Poetry Wall

In front of a wall
I meditated.
The poets from various countries wrote verses on the wall
looked like different varieties of vines
climbing thereon.

In order not to tangle with other vines
I was careful
to suppress my vine desire
and control the extended directions of my vine braches.

For let you
straight reach to my heart
I avoided my familiar hieroglyphs
let my vine spread along your Spanish leaves:
 "I am lost
  within the ambiguous labyrinth of your language."

Oh, my Neruda,

your eyes in serious studying projected spring sunshine

to promote the vines blooming,

your admiring tongue generated spring breeze

to push the vines dancing.

Your compassion grew a wonderful vine

intertwined

intertwined with my vine

under the sunshine.

Reciting Metallic Laughter

South American poet recited metallic laughter. [1]

Taiwanese poet recited metallic laughter.

Male poet recited metallic laughter.

Female poet recited metallic laughter.

Laughter induced more laughter

like making confession towards the valley

triggering a sweet response.

Oh, my Neruda,

you are like that poet[2] catching cold to lost his voice,

but from the mouth shape of Chilean friends

I heard your laughter

and saw your smile face.

Chilean friends

frequently cross talked to me with laughter

making those two daze

drowsy fishes

on my eye corners

endeavoring upstream with power.

Ah, the laughter is a golden key

opening the secret door to Heaven.

*[1] "Metallic Laughter" is the title of sixth poem in the book "20 Love Poems to Chile" by poet Lee Kuei-shien.

*[2] Taiwanese poet Lee Kuei-shien lost his voice due to catch cold during the 14th Tras las Huellas del Poeta poetry festival in 2018, so that his poems can only be recited by Chen Hsiu-chen in Mandarin and by El Salvadoran poet Oscar Benítez in Spanish.

Love

To have pregnancy

of love

is wonderful,

please don't use your hands

your lips

to urge the birth of my love.

To have pregnancy

of ambiguous love

is happy,

please don't use your whisper

your spell

to deliver my love.

To have pregnancy

of love

is a beautiful dream not to be awaken,

never be awaken.

The love fingerprints stamp on the belly

not to be hidden anymore.

Oh, my Neruda,

the dystocia of love

and the throes of love

make people feel profoundly

the existence of love.

Where Would I be Delivered

The sunset answered a curtain call,
while the evening clouds traversed the sky
like a white satin ribbon
wrapping the world as an elegant gift.

During the tired journey
my body was hidden deep in the world
stuffed into the car trunk for taking a nap.
My feeling fluctuated all the way
appeared to the moon passing by the mountain.

Time flied in competition
with the speed of night car
never knowing tired.
Time, ah, time
where would I be delivered
and to whom as a gift?

Time ticked

as ceaseless heartbeats.

Oh, my Neruda,

I heard your attractive male voices

having been answering gently:

time always

stays on the side of love.

I am Afraid

A pink smile
makes the rose faded away.

Whether you smile
or not
your glance
will ripple
caused by witch's sneaky kiss.

As I am a rose
I love your smile,
as I am a witch
I love the tenderness of your wavy glance.

No,
I love neither your smile
nor your glance.

Your smile and your glance

are the mistake road signs

causing me a quick turn on the straight avenue.

Oh, my Neruda,

the secret road leads me to illusory misty clouds.

I am expecting

yet I am afraid

that any ferocious lion

waits at strange mountain path.

That Day

That day
I wanted to dive hidden into the sea,
I wanted to fly concealed into the cloud.
You wanted to catch my feet
and break my wings.

That day
I walked on the shore of once tsunami
with cold wind like a wild beast.
I examined the beach against the wind
hoped to pick up one shell
full filling with sea song
in memory of the history of meeting you on the horizon.
The collections carefully stored in the beach
are one by one promise
already placed into the pockets of many couples.

Oh, my Neruda,

I am afraid

that day will be similar to that one shell

buried in many thousand sands of time

keeping me from searching.

Cold

In deep night of early spring
I pulled on winter coats one by one
like an onion
buried into a thick quilt as black soil
waiting for sunrise
let me sprout.

Oh, my Neruda,
before I sprout
please extend your thick hands quickly
for I want to hold
a warm spring.

The cold seawater in Isla Negra
trembles in waiting
the sun as flame
to boil
love.

Moving Forward to Vicuña

The car instead of horse

moved forward to Vicuña.

The stone mountains around exposed real scenery

only the trees nearby broke out of the dungeon.

The sun treated stone mountains as it experimental canvases

to change colors depending on at dawn or at dusk.

Across over many hills

I haven't seen one bird nor heard its song.

The poet* points out for me the blue lake in the valley.

The lake is bent due to the mountains

sometime invisible

sometime visible.

Change over many thoughts

I probably passed by a lot of

hawthorns or carobs

apricots or fig forests.

Finally we arrived at Vicuña when the stone mountains

at dusk turned into transparent pale violet.

Oh, my Neruda,

I didn't become that lake unable flowing to the sea

or that tree doing nothing but absent minded.

I have experienced many lonely sunsets

and finally arriving at the land of poets.

If you are a stone mountain

I will turn into a seed

to be planted into your body

becoming your bone.

Your Love

Your love

is so ambiguous

that only at real time

may stay on my hand temporary

like a migratory bird

and pull off some feathers for me

to defend by myself against long winter season.

Your love

is so tender

and sweet,

you use the letters with body temperature

to embrace me tightly

across mountains and seas, passing over time and space.

Your love

is so tremendous

that stuffed within my body,

the universe in which I am living.

I breathe your love

all the time.

Your love

is so wonderful

that when I can't see you

I can feel your existence,

when I can't hear you

my heartbeat sounds like drumbeat

going on proceeding the pilgrimage toward you.

Your love

is so cruel

that when I decide to give up loving you

you will suddenly appear

causing my fragile eyes
impossibly closed or turned away.

Your love
is so merciful
that become my only elixir
when I get hurt or sick
because you.

Oh, my Neruda,
please extend your holy hands
to baptize me before my healing.
I pray to be
your sole follower.

My Piety

Oh, my Neruda,

I use your letters to braid a magic scarf

for folding my own feeling,

I use your letters to weave a handkerchief

for wiping my tears and my blood,

I use your letters to stack a cloudy mountain

for meditation,

I use your letters to build a monastery

for Dharma discussion behind closed doors,

I use your letters to pave the road

for courtesy with thrice kneeling and nine kowtows.

Creeping

under the indifferent sky

I kiss the earth that sometimes too icy

and sometimes hot,

such as kissing your toes.

Why your tender letters

are turned into stones

wearing my knees hurtful.

My forehead appears black dead skin due to bowing,

I endure my pains

to go on kneeling and kowtow

until the sky and earth darkened

because you are ahead.

You are ahead

far away on the remote opposite bank

calling to me

indistinctly.

Love Event

The Aurora
in the dark sky
ignites green fireworks,
no star finds it
no one makes witness
even the sky without eyes
cannot see it.

The floret
emerges desperately
from the bush prison.
No nightingale sees the floret sniggering,
no butterfly smells the floret dispersing fragrance.
The big tree without ears
cannot hear the sound of
flower blooming.

The fisherman

hooks full of love spirit foods

sinking into the hungry river.

Drifting clouds float on water

one, two, three...

no single fish eye notices it.

Oh, my Neruda,

one after another gust of wind

has gone,

it seems no love event

has happened.

The Dream

The dream, a little beast
with charms,
is favored like a rose.

I hug him,
kiss him,
I caress him,
feed him the starry sky all night.
He is my sole pet.

The dream
chews the stars
one, two, three...
He starts to take possession of
your twinkling starry eyes.

Oh, my Neruda,

now his eyes glow brightly.

I am starting to see clearly

that he has your rose red lips

and soft hair in night shade.

What most important is

his hands learn to follow your syntax.

I swear that

he is the most powerful poet

with words as his weapons.

Sometimes

he hides in the jungle for a joke

let me impatient

since I am getting more blind.

Oh, my Neruda,

the dream fangs finished chewing the starry sky all night

then turned around to chew

the Adam's ribs deserted to me

that makes me a drastic pain

indescribable.

You Are

You are the starlight.
At dark night without visible stars
I took out from my heart the verses
which is yellowish like lemon juice,
because I knew
the stars will light up again
the splattered inky night.

You are a mountain
planted with red, yellow and white
skin colored roses,
there are also thorns of sorrow,
anyway, the wind will blow me towards the mountain.
No one understands me
coming to watch the maple trees stripped off all red leaves,
but without despair

because I feel confident that

the grass will sprout from black soil after winter snow.

You are an ocean

possessing variable aspects of Cubism.

Your language will upsurge the waves,

thousands of fishes which worship you

swim to become a lot of comma.

I pray to be an ocean myself

extending ten million hands out of waves

to cover you as a fish

gently,

covering you under

my unpredictable mysterious whirlpool.

Admiration of Light, No.1

In jungle

the fireflies flash florescent light.

I see the light of hope

that will be spread by warmth.

I am moving my footsteps forward

to find the hillsides where light spots gather.

Faint light spots are suddenly hunted by

millions of backlit hands

while the eyes toward to light

are hunted by

millions hands of injustice.

On this page

the fluorescent light in history goes out

and the light in my eyes goes out too.

Oh, my Neruda,

the universe is so dark

that I try to extend my hands

into your poetry

to catch

happy fluorescent light.

Will you declare a vindication for me?

Admiration of Light, No.2

"Among the darkness
you should be the fluorescence."
This is the only will
that every firefly would like to leave
to the admirer of light.

In front of the darkness
someone extinguishes the tinder in his heart
to become a black wall.

Oh, my Neruda,
you lived in a stable life,
Spain is in your heart*.
You countered against a great dark age
by means of a bit of fluorescence.
In your fluorescence
I think

how to become a firefly.

Taiwan is in my heart

In a trance

I heard a revelation

announced by prophets of firefly :

for exploration of the progress of the firefly's mental

do not retreat from

inheriting firefly's mental.

On a dark background

I gradually recognize

who generates fluorescence

to illuminate the black wall.

*Neruda's poetry entitled with "Spain in Our Heart".

A Different Me

My hands remain floral fragrance
un-washable
by millions times of washings.

Experienced with frosty seasons
my body keeps memory of
the temperature in hot summer.

My eyes
saw through falling leaves, rains and snows
and countless sunsets
reaching the sweetest time.

My ears
heard repeatedly
the voices always the same.
I finally learned to sing in solo

your love song
and forget many more
other melodies in the world.

Oh, my Neruda,
when the world is dumb
and in dispute
I sing the lyric
that you taught me
until the red rose blooms
in full universe.

If

If you present me the earrings
I will imagine
Zeus fishing on the starry sky all night
with a crescent moon as gold hook.

If you present me the ring
I will imagine
the smallest donut
or the handcuff hardest to get rid of
in the fairy tale.

If you present me fresh flowers
I will imagine
a rose blooming in your garden
with the fragrance of
a poem I have written for you.

Oh, my Neruda,

even if you present me the whole world

which is no more than

your inseparable embrace.

If you ask me for a gift

I have nothing to present

except

an over sensitive heart.

The Quilt

The quilt
incubates a vast starry sky.
Every star represents an old sheep
one star, two stars, three stars...
Each star becomes a letter
representing one of your poems
for hypnosis
and hypnosis again.

Under the starry sky
large tectonic plates jams
to cause me shifted.
But I never learn
to understand the unclear star map.

The quilt
analyzes the dream of its owner

to make full understanding of his mind
and provide the warmth necessary for him.

Oh, my Neruda,
you are on the opposite bank of the Pacific Ocean,
where the starry sky twinkles at Isla Negra in spring,
you don't understand loneliness of the quilt.

Cruel Lovers

Night sky is a grand prison
to imprison the moon child,
all stars blink innocent eyes, obviously
willing to be as female prisoners.

In the concentration camp of garden
the children of trees and herbs are imprisoned,
while the flowers are obviously pleasant
to have heavy makeup respectively
striving for favor of people and God.

The fences along coast
stop the waves from coming ashore
but the waves clap in chorus
with the shore day and night.

Oh, my Neruda,
the lovers walk hand in hand
through so cruel scenery
without a little bit of mercy
within their hearts.

In Love

I looked at the purple mountain
in the distance
hearing the cacti over there
praying with humble wishes for blooming.

As a happy prisoner
I was repeatedly locked into the car
while the tireless waves
slap black and white rocks as piano keys.

Oh, my Neruda,
your hands, for writing peerless love poems
and for revolution by means of letters
trying to change the fate of the country,
change instead my destiny inadvertently.

As a knight

you embrace me.

In your embrace I feel endless sorrow.

The river will flow to its own ocean

and clouds will drift back to their own mountain depressions.

In sorrow

I feel love

present

thus learn in love from the stars

to radiate shines.

Christmas Gifts

Santa Claus
carried a big red bag
full filled with blessing gifts
sledding through the heavy snowstorms and
sliding down the chimney pipe accompanied with jingle bells.

Time sounds tick-tack tick-tack
as the voices of heartbeat
I'm afraid falling asleep for waiting too long.

Modern Santa Claus
emerges out of the internet
with his big red bag
full filled with happy words
wish you, you and you rich.

People need no longer to spend time
in dressing up a Christmas trees
and also no longer to wait for
the gifts packed with butterfly knots.
The pocket moneys for celebration will fall from the sky,
more than raindrops in rainy season,
more than faded petals from cherry blossoms.

With the big fortune of great money
you can buy thousands socks to receive the gifts.
Who will care Christmas,
who will care
the slow motion of Santa Claus.

The footsteps of Santa Claus are
sometimes closer and other far away.
Oh, my Neruda,

I wait patiently in the cold night

for you, the Christmas gift that

I begged to the God days and nights.

Gabriela Mistral's Old House

At former simple house of Gabriela Mistral
I imagined a literary giant
in her youth life and living circumstances.

In remote mountain
the citizens of Vicuña cannot imagine
the poor girl born in the mountain area
will be the winner of Nobel Prize in Literature
no more difficult than picking a lemon from the tree.

Living along with the trees in front of the court
layered stone mountains
silent sky
simple and passionate people in mountain villages
ah, poor Mistral,
your betrayed lover committed suicide...

the story of your life is like these tortuous roads

in the mountain area.

Love is

harder to win than Nobel prize in literature.

How many tears have been wept

in writing your Sonnets of Death*,

I secretly wiped off your grief

that your tears have wetted

my heart.

* "Sonnets of Death", a poetry book written by Gbriela Mistral for her
  suicide lover.

At Museo Gabriela Mistral

Photos, poetry books, cultural relics...
belonging to Gabriela Mistral
now becomes the public assets shared with all people.

Even if the letters form an inapprehensible gap
and the images on photos have been faded
light and shadow of old ages
can be captured without doubt.

At window sill
the bust statue of Gabriela Mistral
has been placed opposite to a group picture of children
highlighting her image as a school teacher.
I sat beside her and looked up
feeling that this gloomy statue
is projecting an incomparable energy.

The spring breeze in Vicuña city
blew through the window sill
caressing her face
also my face.

I brought Gabriela Mistral
stored in my heart, back to Taipei
while left the statue behind in Vicuña.

Dreamland

——To poet Vicente Huidobro*[1]

You and me are separated
with a layer of thin soil.
No,
it is separated with a layer of sleeping
or a dream.

I am restrained
outside the door,
it cannot be opened even by thousands of keys.
You said: "Let the verse opens a thousand doors".

I hear the fallen leaves
still falling in your poem
fluttering.
I'm shaken in my heart.

Throw away the lifeless adjectives,[2]

praise instead nightingale

let it sing loudly in the jungle of poetry,

chant bees

let the honey slip from the text

Oh, poet

you are a little god.[3]

I wish

to live in your genesis.

[1] Vicente Huidobro (1893~1948), a famous Chilean poet, the proponent
of creativeism.

[2] Vinson Vidovro in his poem "Arte poética" advocates abandoning
adjectives.

[3] Vinson Vidovro concluded "The poet is a little God" at the end of his
poem "Arte Poética".

I Devoted the Rose

——To Óscar Castro

I hold a red rose

since you lived with brilliant roses.

Even stronger wind

cannot blow away your prayer.

Your poems have been composed*

to make your romance

sung throughout the streets in Chile.

Among the lily's fragrance under moonlight

your loneliness

exactly has kissed

my loneliness.

I devoted the rose

to accompany you

in your sound sleep.

Your soul is brimming with tears,

how can I forget you?

Your name is the poet

Óscar Castro.

* Óscar Castro 's poem "Para Que No Me Olivides".

Fantasia, No.1

The fishes of eyes
swim on the island of the face,
swim and swim,
never reaching
the uphill of the nose.
Tears drip down constantly.

Oh, my Neruda,
The distance is so short
while the yearning is too long.

Fantasia, No.2

Who

carries a sunset lantern

towards the mountain depression

towards the sea abyss

looking for lost stars?

Oh, my Neruda,

the stars never disappear

just turned to azure

expecting to see

how you are missing.

Fantasia, No.3

All stars in the sky

collectively stay at Bodhimanda all night

in meditation,

always meditate

to become the moon

to become the sun.

Oh, my Neruda,

you are in my heart

staying at the secret Bodhimanda in meditation

meditation

meditation… …

The Way of Thinking

By paving the way of thinking

word by word,

I stand among the words

lingering among the sentences

and settling in verses

to find the meaning of life.

I hid among the words

holding my breath

listening to your breathing heartbeats.

I can feel you

as joy as a seagull

as sad as a black reef.

Between you and me

it communicates

word by word.

Each poem causes a unified mouth shape

calling the same name

Neruda.

Oh, my Neruda.

Chilean Spring Grass

Don't be treated as useless weed
you bloom the flower
among the weeds.

Don't be imprisoned in a vase
you transform at your best from flowers
into a capsular fruit
filled with honey of life.

The sweet taste
is transferred from fruits to flowers
while the fragrance atmosphere
from flowers to branches and leaves.

My endeavor is so hard
that let you realize my efforts.

Oh, my Neruda,

have your turn your gaze to me?

When you stare

at my body

I am no longer merely a fruit.

Transit

Waves, windbreak forests

… … … …

The landscape has no protagonist.

The wasteland waits for spring

never rest, even sleep

till the spring

blushes with big heartbeats.

The abandoned railway

waits for no train.

I am waiting for you here.

Who will be late,

you or me?

Oh, my Neruda,

the spring will be eventually blown away by summer wind.

The clock pushes forward the calendar,

the calendar pushes forward the romance.

I put my ears against the faint drum

trying my best

to prevent my black hair turned to white.

Oh, My Neruda

Oh, my Neruda,

you prevent me to look clear

the figure of age

on my clock face.

And you have reported wrong time

every hour.

Oh, my Neruda,

You are instead of my mirror

making me confused to distinguish

between your face and my face.

I make up with smile every moment

to keep your face

in coincidence with my face.

Oh, my Neruda,

You blocked my mouth with your tongue.

In the small world

it is no longer to separate black from white.

Your lip stands for my heart

to declare.

How Can You

You circle your arms

as a harbor

as a necklace

as a pair of handcuffs.

The spring

opens its sunny mouth

to suck all moistures

from my whole body.

Oh, my Neruda,

how can you

set fire on my eyes.

No more tears

are able to extinguish

the flames burning on my body.

Pale Purple

At dusk

the stone mountain reveals transparent pale purple.

I grow my wings of fantasy.

Under the moonlight

I fly into your eye sockets

to construct nests.

At midnight

I'm blown into your dream to take an adventure.

Your bow and arrows are laid aside apparently,

why I was injured all over my body.

Oh, my Neruda,

you are the hunter getting something for nothing

and I must be healed deep in your

soul.

Anti-drug

When I entered into Chile

the dog detector on duty in a face of justice

went around my luggage

sniffing.

Does

its lungs prefer my perfume?

When I departed Chile

the anti-drug dog

took attention with serious nostrils

staring at my luggage

smelling

thoughtfully.

Oh, my Neruda,

confronting with severe scrutiny by the authorities

my heart is disturbed

since I was smuggling a kiss
really in my luggage.

About the Poet

Chen Hsiu-chen, graduated from Department of Chinese Literature in Tamkang University and has been served as an editor in newspaper and magazines, now is one of the editor members of "Li Poetry Sociaty". Her publications include essay *"A Diary About My Son, 2009"*, poetry *"String Echo in Forest, 2010"*, *"Mask, 2018"*, *"Uncertain Landscape, 2017"*, *"Tamsui poetry, 2018"* and *"BoneFracture, 2018"* as well as Mandarin-English-Spanish trilingual *"Promise, 2017"*.

Her poems have been selected into Mandarin-English-Spanish trilingual anthologies *"Poetry Road Between Two-Hemispheres, 2015"* and *"Voices from Taiwan, 2017"*, Spanish *"Opus Testimoni, 2017"*, Italian *"Dialoghi, 2017"* and *"Quaderni di traduzione, 2018"*, as well as English *"Whispers of Soflay, Vol. 2, 2018"* and *"Amaravati Poetic Prism, 2018"*. Her poems have been also translated into Bengali, Albanian, Turkish and the like.

She participated Formosa International Poetry Festivals in Taiwan held in 2015~2019 annually, Kathak International Poets Summit in Dhaka, Bangladesh, 2016, International Poetry Festival "Ditët e Naimit" in Tetova, Macedonia, 2016, Capulí Vallejo y su Tierra in Peru, 2017, International Poetry Festival of Sidi Bou Saïd Tunisia, 2018, "Tras las Huellas del Poeta"in Chile, 2018, 3rd International Poetry Festival in Hanoi, Vietnam, 2019, 6thIasi International Poetry Festival in Romania, 2019, as well as Primer Festival Internacional de Poesía por Ediciones El nido del fénix, 2019. She was awarded with estrella matutina by Festival of Capulí Vallejo y su Tierra in Peru, 2018. Lebanon Naji Naaman Literary Prizes 2020.

About the Translator

Lee Kuei-shien (b. 1937) began to write poems in 1953, became a member of the International Academy of Poets in England in 1976, joined to establish the Taiwan P.E.N. in 1987, elected as Vice-President and then President of it, and served as chairman of National Culture and Arts Foundation from 2005 to 2007. Now, he is Vice President for Asia in Movimiento Poetas del Mumdo (PPdM) since 2014, the organizer of Formosa International Poetry Festival. His poems have been translated and published in Japan, Korea, Canada, New Zealand, The Netherlands, Yugoslavia, Romania, India, Greece, USA, Spain, Brazil, Mongolia, Russia, Latvia, Cuba, Chile, Nicaragua, Bangladesh, Macedonia, Turkey Poland, Serbia, Portugal, Malaysia, Italy, Mexico and Morocco.

Published works include *"Collected Poems"* in six volumes, 2001, *"Collected Essays"* in ten volumes, 2002, *"Translated Poems"* in eight volumes,

2003, "*Anthology of European Poetry*" in 25 volumes, 2001~2005, "*Elite Poetry Series*" in 38 volumes, 2010~2017, and others in total more than 200 books. His poems in English translation include "*Love is my Faith*", 1997, "*Beauty of Tenderness*", 2001, "*Between Islands*", 2005, "*The Hour of Twilight*", 2010, "*20 Love Poems to Chile*", 2015, "*Existence or Non-existence*", 2017, and "*Sculpture & Poetry*", 2018. The book "*The Hour of Twilight*" has been translated into English, Mongol, Russian, Romanian, Spanish, French, Korean, Bengali, Serbian, Albanian and Turkish, and yet to be published in Macedonian, German, and Arabic languages.

Awarded with Merit of Asian Poet, Korea (1993), Rong-hou Taiwanese Poet Prize, Taiwan (1997), World Poet of the Year 1997, Poets International, India (1998), Poet of the Millennium Award, International poets Academy, India (2000), Lai Ho Literature Prize, Taiwan (2001) and Premier Culture Prize, Taiwan (2002). He also received the Michael Madhusudan Poet Award from the Michael Madhusudan Academy, India (2002), Wu San-lien Prize in Literature, Taiwan (2004), Poet Medal from Mongolian Cultural Foundation, Mongolia (2005), Chinggis Khaan Golden Medal for 800th Anniversary of Mongolian State, Mongolia (2006), Oxford Award for Taiwan Writers, Taiwan (2011), Award of Corea Literature, Korea (2013), Kathak Literary Award, Bangladesh (2016), Literary Award "Naim Frashëri", Macedonia (2016), "Trilce de Oro", Peru (2017), National Culture and Arts Prize, Taiwan (2018), Bandera Iluminada, Peru (2018) and Prime Poetry Award for Excellence by Pulitzer Books, India (2019).

He was nominated by International Poets Academy and Poets International in India as a candidate for the Nobel Prize in Literature in 2002, 2004 and 2006, respectively.

語言文學類　PG2408　台灣詩叢13

親愛的聶魯達 My Beloved Neruda
——陳秀珍漢英雙語詩集

作　　　者／陳秀珍（Chen Hsiu-chen）
英語譯者／李魁賢（Lee Kuei-shien）
叢書策劃／李魁賢（Lee Kuei-shien）
責任編輯／林昕平、陳彥儒
圖文排版／周妤靜
封面設計／王嵩賀

發　行　人／宋政坤
法律顧問／毛國樑　律師
出版發行／秀威資訊科技股份有限公司
　　　　　114台北市內湖區瑞光路76巷65號1樓
　　　　　電話：+886-2-2796-3638　傳真：+886-2-2796-1377
　　　　　http://www.showwe.com.tw
劃撥帳號／19563868　戶名：秀威資訊科技股份有限公司
　　　　　讀者服務信箱：service@showwe.com.tw
展售門市／國家書店（松江門市）
　　　　　104台北市中山區松江路209號1樓
　　　　　電話：+886-2-2518-0207　傳真：+886-2-2518-0778
網路訂購／秀威網路書店：https://store.showwe.tw
　　　　　國家網路書店：https://www.govbooks.com.tw

2020年8月　BOD一版
定價：390元
版權所有　翻印必究
本書如有缺頁、破損或裝訂錯誤，請寄回更換

國家圖書館出版品預行編目

親愛的聶魯達My Beloved Neruda：陳秀珍漢英雙語
詩集 / 陳秀珍著. -- 一版. -- 臺北市：秀威資訊科
技, 2020.08
　　　面；　公分. -- (語言文學類；PG2408)(台灣詩
叢；13)
　　BOD版
　　中英對照
　　ISBN 978-986-326-833-8(平裝)

863.51   109010588

讀者回函卡

感謝您購買本書，為提升服務品質，請填妥以下資料，將讀者回函卡直接寄回或傳真本公司，收到您的寶貴意見後，我們會收藏記錄及檢討，謝謝！
如您需要了解本公司最新出版書目、購書優惠或企劃活動，歡迎您上網查詢或下載相關資料：http:// www.showwe.com.tw

您購買的書名：＿＿＿＿＿＿＿＿＿＿＿＿＿＿＿＿＿＿＿＿＿

出生日期：＿＿＿＿年＿＿＿＿月＿＿＿＿日

學歷：□高中 (含) 以下　　□大專　　□研究所 (含) 以上

職業：□製造業　□金融業　□資訊業　□軍警　□傳播業　□自由業
　　　□服務業　□公務員　□教職　　□學生　□家管　　□其它＿＿＿

購書地點：□網路書店　□實體書店　□書展　□郵購　□贈閱　□其他

您從何得知本書的消息？

　□網路書店　□實體書店　□網路搜尋　□電子報　□書訊　□雜誌

　□傳播媒體　□親友推薦　□網站推薦　□部落格　□其他＿＿＿＿＿

您對本書的評價：（請填代號　1.非常滿意　2.滿意　3.尚可　4.再改進）

　封面設計＿＿＿　版面編排＿＿＿　內容＿＿＿　文／譯筆＿＿＿　價格＿＿＿

讀完書後您覺得：

　□很有收穫　□有收穫　□收穫不多　□沒收穫

對我們的建議：＿＿＿＿＿＿＿＿＿＿＿＿＿＿＿＿＿＿＿＿＿

＿＿＿＿＿＿＿＿＿＿＿＿＿＿＿＿＿＿＿＿＿＿＿＿＿＿＿＿＿

＿＿＿＿＿＿＿＿＿＿＿＿＿＿＿＿＿＿＿＿＿＿＿＿＿＿＿＿＿

11466
台北市內湖區瑞光路 76 巷 65 號 1 樓

秀威資訊科技股份有限公司　　　收

BOD 數位出版事業部

....

（請沿線對折寄回，謝謝！）

姓　　名：＿＿＿＿＿＿＿＿　年齡：＿＿＿＿　性別：□女　□男

郵遞區號：□□□□□

地　　址：＿＿＿＿＿＿＿＿＿＿＿＿＿＿＿＿＿＿＿＿＿

聯絡電話：(日) ＿＿＿＿＿＿＿＿＿＿　(夜) ＿＿＿＿＿＿＿＿＿＿

E-mail：＿＿＿＿＿＿＿＿＿＿＿＿＿＿＿＿＿＿＿＿＿